Anonymous

Mary Lincoln

Home scenes from the life of a young lady

Anonymous

Mary Lincoln
Home scenes from the life of a young lady

ISBN/EAN: 9783337118648

Printed in Europe, USA, Canada, Australia, Japan

Cover: Foto ©Raphael Reischuk / pixelio.de

More available books at **www.hansebooks.com**

MARY LINCOLN:

HOME SCENES

FROM THE

LIFE OF A YOUNG LADY.

CINCINNATI:
ROBERT CLARKE & CO.,
FOR THE AUTHORESS.
1862.

AT YOUR FEET,

MY BELOVED FATHER,

I LAY THESE IMPERFECT THOUGHTS AND FANCIES,

THE FIRST JOTTINGS OF MY PEN.

PREFACE.

THIS little romance was begun to while away the lonely evening hours of a desolate winter. *The first Chapters* were written and laid away, without a thought of the completion of the whole, although the plan had been previously arranged. They were accidentally brought to light and read by a friend, a very "partial judge," who expressed an interest in the story and desired that it should be finished and—published.

At first, I would not listen to sending my very faulty creation afloat; but afterwards, a curiosity to see how it would look in *print*, induced me to consent. I must acknowledge that I have a great many misgivings—that I should fade away in mortification to hear these "fancies," and their style criticised, but as I expect to be incognito, I do not know why I should fear being found out. If you should ever guess the author, please be so kind as to say nothing about it, at least in *her presence*.

CINCINNATI, Feb. 1862.

MARY LINCOLN.

CHAPTER I.

"WHAT a cold, dismal evening this is, mother!" said Mary Lincoln, as she stood between the rich damask curtains of the sitting-room window, and looked out into the cheerless street: "How glad I am that I am not obliged to go out to-night! Heaven pity the poor, this comfortless season! Why! there goes the same woman who was here, begging, this morning. Mother, do you know her well?" And with this question, Mary, brushing back her curling locks, advanced to her mother's chair.

"Yes, my child," replied Mrs. Lincoln, "I know her well; during many years I have aided her; she is a very worthy object, and were she not, Mary, I should still consider it my duty to do all I could for her. You know our Father maketh his sun to shine on the evil as well as the good, and should we not, striving to imitate him, lend a willing hand to all whom misfortune has overtaken, even to those who are undeserving?"

"I never saw any one so grateful," said Mary, "Amy tells me she is not the only one for whom you care ; she says you are so good, you are *always* doing for those who can not help themselves, and that you do not bestow charity only, but you give with it good counsel and Christian advice. I wish, dear mother, I could asist you in sewing for poor Mrs. Arthur's children ! May I not, mother ? And Mary threw her arms round her mother's neck and kissed her.

" Yes, my daughter," said Mrs. Lincoln, " not just now, but when you are a year or two older, you shall join me in this work of love and charity."

" A year or two older?" said Mrs. Lincoln sadly to herself, "a year or two more, and my children will be motherless. I shall have passed away, never more to return. Oh ! why at the thought of this parting, am I filled with unspeakable anguish? My Father ! in agony I say, spare, spare me yet a few years ; give to me those hours of pure companionship with my children, in which I should watch their development of body and mind, in which I should cultivate in them whatever is good, and noble, and lovely, in which I should walk hand in hand with them to Heaven. Separate us not yet, I beseech Thee ! But if, O God, I must part from them, and I know I must, I *know* my death knell has already struck, give me strength to leave my precious lambs, (without a sigh, without a fear for their future,) entirely in Thy hands."

Mrs. Lincoln with an effort stifled back the unhappy thoughts which lately had so occupied her, and with a smile she said to Mary, " Yes my love, it will be delightful to sit and sew with you, and when your young fingers tire, you shall read to me, and we shall be so happy, shall we not my child?"

Mary looked into her mother's face; she thought her cheerful words seem forced; she pushed back the drooping lace which shaded her mother's soft cheek; the cheek was full, was delicately tinged, the eyes were bright, and clear, and beaming.

Afterwards, how often memory recalled to Mary Lincoln, that quiet evening, and that mournful tone.

" But, my darling," said Mrs. Lincoln, " you forget your piano has been untouched to-day; will you not practice this evening? But first ring the bell for Robert, or call him, if you please."

" Yes, dear mother, I will," said Mary, and she bounded across the soft carpet, through the hall and the dining-room, into the servants' parlor, where sat the domestic she was seeking. " Robert," said she, " Mamma wishes to see you in the sitting-room, if you please—and you, darling little Birdie," addressing her only sister, Bertha, nine years younger: " Dear little lambkin, don't you want to hear sister· play those beautiful waltzes you like so well?"

Bertha jumped out of her nurse's lap, " her Kitty," as she called her, and dancing up to her sister seized her hand and went skipping along with her into the sitting-room. Mary now took her seat at the piano, while Robert lighted the gas and put fresh coals on the fire. Mrs. Lincoln drew down the folds of the rich crimson curtains, until they swept the floor, shutting out darkness and rain; glanced at the small French clock which stood on the black marble mantelpiece, and as she sat she said :

"Robert, you may serve our little supper here, Mr. Lincoln will not be at home this evening."

Robert bowed and withdrew.

Kitty came to take Bertha, but her mamma said, "Not yet, Kitty," whereupon Bertha gave one light bound, and so sprang into her mother's arms. The mother laid the bright face, with its beautiful features, its soft clear complexion, its long silken lashes, shading those magnificent eyes, the ringletted head against her bosom, she took the small hand in hers, she folded the little figure close to her heart, and kissed the sweet pouting lips ; she kissed the rosy cheeks, she kissed the eyelids, the lovely brow, and the child looked up in her face and smiled.

And while the young fingers at the piano drew forth melodious murmurings ; or strains like sparkling cascades, rushing, leaping, foaming, tumbling; or mournful cadences, in whose "lengthened swell," "grief seemed lingering," the mother sat and forgetting the dread of her life, gave herself up to the luxury of that hour.

Memory went back to the birth hours of her children; she dwelt still shrinkingly on their awful agony ; then on the calm of body and of soul which succeeded; then the tide of sweet, ecstatic bliss, which swept over her when for the first time the little, soft, helpless immortal was laid in her arms ; she recalled the tremor of delight as the tiny being nestled close to her ; the tears that came flowing swiftly down her cheek when the first tooth made its appearance; the first tottling step, the first attempted word, and all the winning ways of babyhood; her grief when the babe suffered, her fear of losing it; her lonely night-watches over the couch, perhaps of death.

Then she thanked God with her whole heart that he had spared her children thus far to her, and she thanked Him for that most deep, most pure, most holy love, never growing cold, never ceasing, seeking always the highest good, the highest happiness of its object.

And as the sweet gushes of maternal love welled up into her heart, throbbing in every pulse of her being, she inwardly exclaimed, "How rich! how rich I am! O God, I thank thee for my children; let not my love for them absorb every other love; in loving them let me not forget Thee!"

And while the clock ticked almost inaudibly in the pauses those young musical fingers made, the little Bertha, in her mother's arms, looked with her magnificent eyes into the fire, and at her mother, and again into the fire, until the lids drooped with the sleep that stole over them, and the long silken eyelashes rested in sound slumber on the blooming cheek. Mrs. Lincoln drew her child still closer, and as she gazed on her wonderful beauty, in visions she saw her passing on through infancy, youth and maidenhood. She knew the thorns of life would prick and scratch this sensitive nature, thus far nurtured in the atmosphere of love, of sympathy, of affection, and being conscious of this she had always fostered the love of her children for each other, saying, "May not this tie between them be all that shall brighten their young lives when I am gone? May not each heart be a shelter for the other, when all earthly things else shall fail?"

Mr. Lincoln was an indulgent husband and father. Every comfort and luxury that money could procure were lavished on his wife and children. Noble by nature, and generous to both friend and foe, *kind* at all times, and sometimes *affectionate* to those he loved, he was yet so absorbed in the accumulation of wealth, that he sacrificed everything to its pursuit—time, religion, intellect, and affection.

Mrs. Lincoln was often pained at the seeming neglect of her husband; neglect she could scarcely call it, but she saw him so seldom, and her heart yearned for hours of communion with him, delightful hours she had known and loved to recall—times, past to return no more, she feared, as long as herself and children were secondary objects in his busy mind.— And in jealousy of spirit would she exclaim:

"He loves me as man loves woman—less than the ends life lives for."

And ashamed of this inward suspicion, she would accuse herself of ill-humor, of fretfulness, of selfishness. Then putting aside her own feelings entirely, she would ponder upon his relation to his children, and dread the future; and then their relation to him. They scarcely knew their father, and she felt how necessary it was they should be acquainted. Then she had asked him pleadingly for more of his presence;

she had told him that his great mercantile success ought not to be a plea for increasing absorption of time and talents in more extended business pursuits. But Mrs. Lincoln did not realize how fascinating was the accumulation of wealth, and that, like many others, the more her husband gained, the more he desired. Hope slowly but gradually died out of her sad heart. Once she had even ventured so far as to tell him her fears for her health, her dread of leaving her children almost strangers to him, but how had he replied to her? He had pushed back the hair from her forehead, looked into her glittering eyes, noted the bright flush on her cheek, and laughed loud, even merrily, and said:

"Nonsense, my love! you mustn't give way to such foolish thoughts. You're good for twenty-five years yet—and as to the children, I know they're very timid with me; but soon, my dear, I do assure you, I hope to spend more time with them and you; and as soon as I can arrange some affairs I have on hand, which perplex me extremely, *then* I shall make you all realize how much I love you, as, indeed, I do, truly."

But the perplexing affairs were never arranged, or if they were, others sprang up in their place, and still Mrs. Lincoln's health became gradually more feeble, her pulse more feverish, her step more faltering, and no one observed it or knew it but herself—and the hopes she had vainly laid on man turned away to God, to Him who faileth not; to Him she gave herself and her children, and in His love and in His power felt full peace and full security.

As these accustomed thoughts passed through her mind the clock kept time to the breath of the slumbering child in her arms.

But the door opened, and the silver tea-tray with its refreshing accompaniments was brought in by Robert, placed on the little round table, and drawn up to the side of the mistress. Kitty noiselessly entered, stole away her precious burden with the warm farewell kiss of its mother on its cheek, bore it off to its chamber, where, all awaiting it, were its bowl of bread and milk; its pretty white night-dress on a chair by the fire; its beautiful bed all open to receive it.

Kitty dearly loved her little charge. Since the birth of Bertha she had faithfully tended her and felt many a pang at the thought of quitting her, and often almost regretted that she had promised to take upon herself the vows which would force her far away from her friends and from this darling child. But she had no time to indulge her grief, for Bertha was now wide awake and all ready for her supper, and then for her white little bed. The supper eaten, the prayer repeated; last of all, "Oh Father! make me a good girl. Bless father, mother, sister, and my Kitty, too;" the sweet good-night embrace given; the "bon soir ma chère Kitty," said; the snow-white bedclothes tucked nicely in; the lovely head laid on the soft pillow; the beautiful limbs stretched out in repose, the little Bertha in two minutes slept soundly.

" So the young bird, when done its twilight lay
  Of praise, folds peacefully at shut of day
  Its head, beneath its wing, and sinks to rest. "

"Come, my daughter, tea is all ready ; and,"—

"Yes, mamma ; I am all ready too,"

And Mary drew up a chair to the round-table, poured out a cup of tea for her mother, and helped herself to her tumbler of iced milk.

Robert placed the silver bell at the hand of his mistress, and quitted the room.

It was Mrs. Lincoln's rule to dispense with her servants at meal time, unless their presence was absolutely necessary. At such hours, the family circle, when not enlarged by visitors, was sacred, neither curious eyes nor ears being allowed to intrude. At present, Mary and her mother had much to talk about. Christmas was approaching, and this interesting subject was to be the evening's theme. It had already been decided that Mary was to have a Christmas tree, and to invite her most intimate friends with their parents, and to present to each person a Christmas token. These had all previously been selected, and now was to be made out the long list of *humble* friends, for whom to provide suitable gifts, and as soon as the light meal was dispatched and the debris taken away, Mrs. Lincoln and Mary set themselves diligently about their work.

Paper and pencil were brought, and Mary drew up more closely to the small round table, and read as she wrote. First of all down on the list went, " Christ-

mas dinners, and a dollar each for all of mamma's pro-
teges."

" That part of the work is very quickly done, Mary," said Mrs. Lincoln.

" All we have to furnish is the money and send Robert to market for a number of turkeys and their accompaniments, and as your father has most nobly
filled my largest purse and given me a check beside,
that, with the money I had already laid away for the
purpose, will be more than amply sufficient for all our
purchases. If to-morrow be a bright day, we must
buy the dresses and shawls for poor Bridget Carey
and Ann Prather, and instead of getting suits of
clothes for Bridget's two little boys, as I first intended, I will give her the money and let her select them
for herself."

And then, down on the list went " shawls and
dresses for Bridget Carey and Ann Prather," and innumerable other articles followed in such quick suc-
cession, that Mary laughingly exclaimed,

" Dear mother, I declare, my arm begins to ache,
and I have almost used up my paper."

" Well, my darling," said Mrs. Lincoln, " I think we
are quite through with this part of our duty, at least,
I know of nothing more in the dry-goods line to be
added."

After a little more discussion, and a little more
reading of the list, Mrs. Lincoln concluded it was
satisfactory, and proceeded to enumerate Mary's
friends, and Bertha's also, not forgetting the maturer
ones, whom she wished to invite to the Christmas

party. There were, Caroline Thomas, the same age as Mary; Gertrude Clifford, three years her senior; Kate Lee, the merry Kate, just her age; and Mary Lovell, two months younger.

Mrs. Lincoln watched very tenderly over her children, and in no respect was her solicitude so great for them as in the choice of their companions.

The queen-like Carrie Thomas, not only remarkable for her dignity, her heaven-like face, her majestic figure, the gentleness and elegance of her manner, but the purity of her heart and life; Gertrude Clifford, just sixteen, the gifted, the beautiful Gertrude, fascinating every one who looked upon her, or listened to her sweet voice; motherless, but with a father who adored her; Kate Lee,

> "Whose heart was like a nest of singing birds
> Rocked on the topmost bough of life."

Mary Lovell, serene, quiet,

> "Like a soft landscape of mild earth, budding and beautiful."

These were friends to love, admire and cherish, and Mrs. Lincoln looked upon them with fond pride and affection, and cultivated the intimacy between them and her daughter.

Mary Lincoln had not one tithe of the beauty of either of her companions, but she had a perfect figure, a luxurious mass of rich soft black hair, teeth like pearls, eyes into whose soft depths you could look far down, eyes in whose gaze the soul was present; a manner so lady-like, so lovely, so kind and

2

forgetful of self, and above all, a heart so good, that
when you looked at her, a stranger, at first glance,
you would say, "not at all pretty," then at the
second, "how sweet, how superior she is."

Mary often contrasted herself with her young
friends, and sometimes she repined, and wondered in
her great yearning for the beautiful, why God had
not made her fair also.

But if classic features and clear complexion had
been denied her, already she knew a beautiful inward
world had been given: a world in which there was
exquisite happiness, and often and again she would
say musingly those lines of her favorite poet,

> "Unseen companions, guests of air
> You can not wait on, will be there;
> They taste not food, they drink not wine,
> But their soft eyes look into mine,
> And their lips speak to me, and all
> The vast and shadowy banquet hall
> Is full of looks and words divine!"

And inwardly exulting, would she thank God for the
"power that dwelt in her bosom, that stirred her inmost soul, that swayed her energies." Mary Lincoln was young in years, but not so young in feeling.

"Mother, are we to dance on Christmas night, or
shall we have a regular frolic instead—charades, for
instance, or old-fashioned games?"

"You are to do just what you please, my daughter. Your father wished me to tell you that you
could have everything your own way; that you must
provide the entertainment, arrange with your own

hands one refreshment table at least, and send for as many musicians as you want, and prepare the evening's programme yourself. He especially desires it, as I do not feel quite strong lately," said Mrs. Lincoln.

"O, dear mother," replied Mary, "I shall be very glad to do all I can, and to relieve you. You must give me your advice, and your judgment and taste, and I will do the rest. And I am sure papa is very kind, and very noble, is he not?"

CHAPTER II.

CHRISTMAS EVE soon came. Mr. Lincoln took tea with his family, leaving immediately after, to attend to some important business.

As many preparations for the morrow evening as could be made in advance, had already been attended to, and Mrs. Lincoln hurried Mary to bed, telling her she must rise early the following morning.

Beside, she had her own work to do after Mary had retired; secret, pleasant, soft steps to take about the house; drawers and closets to open stealthily; large parcels to bring out that had been hidden away, perhaps months—*Christmas parcels*, which the provident care of the mistress had prepared for every one to whom she generally gave at such times.

As soon as they were sure the young folks slept (Kitty smilingly assisted), into Bertha's little bedroom, joining her mother's on one side, first they went, and Santa Claus deposited on a table near the fire-place, a beautiful house already furnished, which Bertha had often on bended knee, looking up the chimney, requested the aforesaid esteemed individual to bring her; and on another table near the bed, dolls, and boxes of blocks, and houses and trees. "Why, little mistress, when you wake, how rich you will find yourself!"

Kitty clasped her hands in delight, anticipating the dear little creature's pleasure, and Mrs. Lincoln smiled gladly.

With a glance at the sleeping child; with finger on her lip, motioning to Kitty, the mistress with her maid left the room. Now they wended their way on tiptoe into the chamber of Mary, joining her mother's on the other side, and in the same manner, with wondering eyes, Kitty helped her mistress bear the Christmas burden, placing it on the center-table in the middle of the room—a magnificent copy of Shakspeare; the Waverly Novels, in their plain rich binding (Mrs. Lincoln's present), and beside them, in a jewel case, a brooch and bracelet of most exquisite pink coral (from Mary's father).

Quitting the room, gently closing the door behind them, Mrs. Lincoln proceeded to give to Kitty her own presents: a handsome black silk dress, which she was to accept from Bertha; a shawl bought for her by Mary; some household articles from herself; a gold piece from Mr. Lincoln. The remaining gifts for the other servants were not to be distributed until morning, when all came in for a goodly share.

The hours were fast passing away, and Mrs. Lincoln, somewhat fatigued, had made her night-toilet, and throwing over all her dressing-gown, went to pay her usual good-night visit to her children. Noiselessly she stepped into the quiet chamber where slept her first born. The flickering fire-light cast its gentle warmth over the luxurious apartment. The roses and lilies, in the medallions of the carpet, when trodden on, almost seemed to breathe out, a soft perfume. On the marble slab under the great mirror fresh flowers bloomed, already prepared for the morrow's festivities.

Rich green curtains, with a bordering of roses of wonderfully exact hues, fell over others of exquisite lace. at the windows; from the ebony and gilt canopy of the French bedstead, drooped others like them, looped back with sprays of crimson leaves. On the mantelpiece were immense bronze candelabra, filled with unlighted wax candles; and a faultless figure of Parian marble, Mary's great delight.

On one side of the room stood Mary's ebony bookcase, filled with her treasures; and on a small table at the foot of her bed were her writing-desk, her Bible, and prayer-book. Over her large arm-chair lay her morning-dress, under it her slippers; everything in the room betokened the neatness and order of the occupant.

Mrs. Lincoln advanced almost breathlessly—she gazed round the beautiful room; she approached the bed, and leaned over the sleeper; she knelt by the bedside, and all a mother's love shone in her face, as looking at the placid features of her tenderly-beloved one, she said:

"Oh, my child, how tranquil thy sleep of youth; untouched by cares, untainted by the world, undisturbed by sorrows! Sleep on, and dream happily whilst thou may. Oh! that thy days might *all* be as calm and as blest as now. Father! hear the midnight prayers of a mother who adores her child. Grant that she may be always as well cared for as now.— Grant that she may never fall into evil. Shield, and protect, and love her, for the sake of Thy Son!"

Slowly she arose and quitted the chamber, and entered the one she had visited once before, to-night. There, nestling in the tiny bed, lay the youngest born. The mother, without fear of waking her, caught and clasped the dimpled hand in hers, and kissed the rich lips, and little Bertha opened her eyes and smiled. Then she turned and slept again, while with a fervent prayer for this darling, too, and a tear of tenderness, Mrs. Lincoln left the room, and, quite fatigued, laid herself down to rest.

CHRISTMAS DAY

Dawned as lovely, as balmy, and as glorious as a May morning. The winter thus far, in this mild climate, had been unusually soft. Roses were still blooming out of doors, and some of the more hardy vines were perfectly green.

Mr. Lincoln's household was very active this morning. At an early hour everything was prepared for the evening, and Mary and her mother, after giving a last look at all the arrangements, expressed their complete satisfaction and admiration of the house, in its holiday garb, and went up stairs to rest. Mrs. Lincoln complimented Mary on her display of taste, particularly in the grouping and placing of the flowers, which had all been made into bouquets early in

the day, as they would keep a long time at this season of the year. In the circular stone vestibule into
which the great hall door opened, were large urns of
blooming roses, and here and there a plant from the
conservatory. On both sides of the broad hall, were
étagères filled with bouquets of exquisite, rare flowers, perfuming all that portion of the house. The
drawing-room (where was hidden the Christmas-tree,
a secret from Bertha, as was also the expected visit
of Santa Claus, in person), was adorned in the same
manner. In the sitting-room, wreaths of mistletoe
and holly, and dark-leaved vines, with red stems and
brown berries, clustered round the picture-frames.—
In the antique silver vases on the black marble mantelpiece, were roses and heliotrope, while heliotrope
and mignonette sent out their combined fragrance in
other parts of the room.

At an early hour the guests assembled, and when
all had arrived, the doors of the grand drawing-room
were thrown open, where, looming up in the darkness
at one end of the large apartment, stood the tall,
graceful Christmas-tree, glittering in the light of its
innumerable wax candles; decorated with birds in
little cages; with gilded nuts; with delicate glass
lanterns, each with its own tiny taper; with rare and
strange bonbons; and under the tree, what quaint
little cattle, almost knee deep in moss; what wonderful little farms and farm-houses!

Bertha and her playmates were in ecstacies of delight.

But, presently, as if by magic, the great chandeliers were lighted, and the older guests, leaving the children to examine the tree, strayed off to another part of the room to look at the fine pictures which hung on the walls.

But soon, shouts of laughter from the young ones, caused every eye to turn inquiringly, when what should they see but a veritable Santa Claus; there he was, sure enough, dressed in his red blouse and shorts, his gray woolen stockings, and slippers with red rosettes upon them, his red hat, his long white beard; and, better than all, round his neck, what strings of toys! and on each side of him large baskets filled with every conceivable thing a child could desire. After an introduction by Mrs. Lincoln to many of the guests, whom he saluted with infinite grace and cordiality, he made a little speech to the children, telling them of his home in Lapland, his reindeer, his recent travels and some of the incidents by the way. As the weather in their climate was so warm, he had found himself obliged to leave his sleigh and deer in Canada, and there borrow of an intimate friend a pair of stout little ponies.

During these remarks, the little ones eyed him with wonder, and fascinated by his pleasant manner gradually drew toward him.

Now he began to distribute his gifts, commencing with the smallest child and continuing until all had received something, even the eldest.

Gertrude Clifford, Kate Lee, and Mary's other friends, were all remembered, and very handsomely, too. As the young girls advanced at the

3

mention of their names, to receive from Santa Claus his offering, many a voice sent forth a low murmur of admiration, predicting a proud future for those lovely young maidens. Now, the soft, subdued music of the band present lent its inspiration to the scene, and for a while old and young joined in the dance. At length supper was announced.

As the guests entered the dining-room, many a whispered encomium was passed, at sight of the table Mary herself had arranged. One lady said to Mrs. Lincoln:

"Mme Monin has fairly eclipsed herself to-night." " Mrs. Lincoln replied, that Madame Monin had not been in this part of the house at all, but had displayed her artistic taste upon the more substantial repast they would find in the breakfast-room, and added that *Mary* had arranged this table with an idea to the pleasure of the children. Mary just then came within hearing of her mother, who said:

"We were just admiring your table, my daughter. Mrs. Phillips desires to engage you for her next party."

"I shall be most happy, dear Mrs. Phillips, to render you my assistance at any time," and with a low bow and a bright smile she flitted away in her cloud of white muslin.

The table *was* prettily adorned. The gas light was not allowed to shine, but the great chandelier was hung with wreaths of holly, and the beautiful rich red and green-leaved ampolopsis. From the silver candelabra, tall white wax candles shed down their soft light on the silver epergnes with their bouquets of white camelias and drooping crimson fuschias; and over the silver fruit-baskets laden with white grapes, and oranges nestling in their own leaves.— Tall pyramids of ices at either end of the table, and in the center a great temple of frosted sugar filled with candied fruits, attracted the attention and commanded the admiration of the youthful part of the company. Crimson cut-glass sparkled on the finest, purest, richest damask table-cloth.

On the white marble mantelpiece, at either end, the silver candelabra, with their crimson and white wax lights, were garlanded with crimson and green leaves, drooping low in graceful festoons over the massive marble, while between them white and red roses bloomed in beauty in their crystal vases.

Quietly observing whether all were well attended to, Mary unobtrusively passed around among the guests. In the breakfast-room she found two gentlemen, discussing a political question over a cold quail. Seeing they had had no coffee, as soon as there was a pause in their conversation, she asked:

"Mr. Lovell, Mr. Phillips, will you have a cup of coffee?"

"No, no, thank you, Miss Mary," said Mr. Lovell, "I never drink coffee; but if you will send one of your agents, with a cup of tea to me, I will drink that, and your health in it, with the greatest pleasure."

"And I, too," said his companion; "I will take a cup of tea, too;" and as Mary turned to order a cup of tea for Mr. Lovell, and one for Mr. Phillips, she heard the two worthy gentlemen go off into a learned disquisition on tea.

Now meeting Robert in another part of the room, she said:

"Robert, please prepare a cup of coffee for mamma —just as she likes it. I think she must be very tired." And presently, with the coffee in her hand, she seeks her mother, and finds her in the dining-room distributing bon-bons to the children. Whisperingly, she says to her, "Dear mother! here is some coffee for you, and an arm-chair in the corner near the fire-place; do come, dear mamma, I am sure you are very tired."

The pale face of Mrs. Lincoln attested the truth of Mary's remark, as she suffered herself willingly to be led away and seated comfortably, while her guests were partaking of her hospitable cheer.

"Shall I get some oysters for you, or some salad, or a quail, mamma?" asked Mary, as she leaned over her mother's chair.

"Nothing, I thank you, dear," said Mrs. Lincoln; "this coffee is good and very refreshing."

Just then, Kitty came with Bertha in her arms—Bertha so sleepy and tired, and going to bed with her great lovely doll.

A group of admiring ladies and children gathered round the darling child, and with a kiss for every one, and two kisses for mamma, and two for papa (who made his appearance at that moment), dear little Miss Bertha went gladly to bed, saying to Kitty:

"What a good Santa Claus he was to-day! wasn't
he, Kitty? and how much I love him for my pretty
dolly!"

After supper, while the musicians were in the dining-room, charades were proposed, which proposal
was warmly seconded. With great alacrity, sides
were chosen, and George May was requested to select
a word as quickly as possible for his party. They
withdrew, and almost immediately returned, some fan-
tastically decked off in anything they could seize on
the instant.

George May now delivered an affectionate speech,
in strong Hibernian dialect, to his followers, who
seemed suddenly to be seized with the deepest love
for each other, talking tenderly, and caressingly
stroking each other on the shoulders. The speech
and its effect caused much merriment among the
lookers-on.

After George and his party had gone out the
second time, they suddenly came in again, one bringing a large wooden arm-chair (Robert's property),
and placing it in the middle of the room. A moment
after, George made his entrance, with an immense
crimson bed-spread pinned under his chin, and a
great book in his hand, and a pair of spectacles far
down over his nose. With great gravity, in his impromptu robe, he ascended his impromptu desk, and
commenced his impromptu sermon. His ridiculous
appearance contrasted so strongly with his earnest
tone and manner, that every one in the room seemed
interested to know what was coming next.

" Dear friends, brothers, and fellow-citizens," he began, as he nervously twitched his spectacles, " Many years ago, long before the birth of Fulton, who, you know, invented steam, that wonderful elastic fluid generated by caloric from that transparent element composed of oxygen and hydrogen, in other words, *water*, my hearers, of which element I shall not particularize, for I am sure you are familiar with the subject—"

" Yes, yes! we know," said his party.

"Silence, my congregation! don't interrupt your speaker.—Then, many years ago, before these days of steam, and railroads, and telegraphs; on the dark ocean, when the heavens were black, and destruction and desolation were sweeping over the earth; when not a living creature was to be seen, nor a leaf, nor a tree—no, not even an insect, and silence, drear and dead silence, reigned, except the descending raindrops, swelling into floods; what like a tiny speck, alone on the wide world, comes riding forth upon the bosom of the mighty waters?"

"Oh, I know," said little Peter Philips, "it was the ark, wasn't it, mother?"

"Oh, yes! the ark! the ark!" exclaimed many young voices at once.

" For further particulars I will refer you to ancient history, my friends;" and adjusting his spectacles, he made a low bow, stepped down from his position with mock dignity, and with great strides left the room, his long gown ridiculously flapping round his heels.

The whole word was next acted out very prettily, and soon the children guessed, " *Patriarch!*"

A grand reel followed, heartily joined in by many; then kind parting words and good nights were said— and the Christmas party at Mr. Lincoln's was over.

CHAPTER III.

A week, a happy week, had passed, spent in the country home of Gertrude Clifford, and Mary Lincoln alighted from the carriage, at her father's house, all impatience to embrace her dear mother.

She was surprised to find the great door ajar, and still more astonished when she gently pushed it open, to see Kitty in the vestibule evidently keeping guard.

"What's the matter, Kitty?" she said. "Do tell me; is any one sick?—is Bertha—"

But Kitty, with raised finger, motioned Mary to silence.

At that moment, Mr. Lincoln came noiselessly forward, and approaching Mary, with a very grave face, led her through the hall into the sitting-room.

"What can it all mean?" she said to herself.

Mr. Lincoln, in almost a whisper, began:

"I have been watching for you all the afternoon, Mary. Your mother is very ill; this morning she ruptured a blood-vessel. The doctor says her life depends upon her perfect quiet—that she *must not* speak, that she *must not* be excited in the least. She is expecting you, and, at your meeting, I caution you to be firm : control all emotion except the pleasure of seeing her again. Do you promise me, Mary ; for I can not let you see her without this promise."

Surprise, grief, but above all an intense desire to be near her dear mother—how *very, very* dear at this moment—filled her young heart, and with many a pang, and a choking back of tears, she bowed an assent to her father, and followed him to the sick chamber.

There, reclining on white pillows, scarcely whiter than her pale face, with closed eyes, lay her dearest, her truest friend. Breathlessly, she glided past the sad attendants, and went round to the other side of the bed. Mrs. Lincoln feebly opened her eyes, and as she saw her child, she smiled a welcome. Mary bent over and kissed her.

But Mr. Lincoln, fearful of the result of this interview, closely followed Mary ; and as if to divert the thoughts of both, began to talk on indifferent subjects, and then to question Mary about her visit at Mr. Clifford's.

But Mary, all this time choking back a heart full of tears, could answer in monosyllables only.

Presently, Mrs. Lincoln made a motion with her right hand, as if she desired something. Her friend, Mrs. Phillips, offered her water, but soon discovered she was looking for her pencil and paper, that had been lying near her.

And as she found them, Mr. Lincoln laughingly turned to Mary, and said, the doctor would allow her mother to communicate with them in *writing* only, and that he intended keeping all her specimens of penmanship and composition in these few days of sickness, as he had no doubt they would be interesting from their variety.

Mary wondered how her father could talk so lightly; she did not see his smothered grief was overwhelming him—that a desperate effort alone enabled him to govern his own feelings.

Mrs. Lincoln laid down her pencil, and handed to Mary the paper upon which she had written.

Mary read: "Pray for me, my daughter!"

Like an electric shock, the consciousness of her mother's immediate danger, rushed upon her, revealing to her also that her mother too fully realized her situation. The thought of forever losing her, overwhelmed her with unspeakable anguish. Tremblingly she clasped the paper, and with a mighty effort she struggled to hide her cruel emotions. She turned with faltering step to quit the chamber of the dying. She passed the threshold. It was too much. A low wail of misery burst from her overcharged young heart, and she fell fainting to the floor. Mr. Lincoln sprang to catch her. Mrs. Lincoln, with a despairing effort, started up, stretched out her arms, sank back—and breathed no more.

Who, with sacrilegious step, dare enter the bereaved household! Who dare lift the vail that conceals sorrowing and desolate hearts! Bowed down with grief at the loss of a dear friend, does not all sympathy fall on us like mockery? Can *any one* feel as we do? Did any one ever lose such a friend as we have lost?

Do those persons who tell us coldly, " It *is* hard to bear, but God means all well, and in time you will see it :"—do *they* know how we writhe in our agony ?—Can they tell how we miss the dear accustomed face, the soft footsteps, the gentle hand laid on our shoulder, the tender light of those loving eyes, the words of sympathy, of encouragement, never to fall on our ears again? These people go out from our dark homes into the sunshine ; the flowers bloom for them, and for them the birds pour forth their sweetest melody, and dear ones wait their return.

We steal out in the shade and in the gloom, while those we loved are gone, gone away forever. No more, in the crowded street, shall we catch the glimpse of that dear familiar face : no more, in the pleasant family circle, does that sweet smile shed its holy light in our hearts !—that empty seat !—that vacant place !

Oh, God ! Oh, God ! have mercy !

Mr. Lincoln mourned, how long! for his wife.—Deep, deep in his heart he buried her image, buried it with the memory of her unvarying kindness, her submission, her attention to his wants and his comforts. Even those memories, too, were soon chilled, and he turned from them, to the end and the aim of his life—making money.

But there were other sorrows, other trials in store for him.

Before the spring flowers blossomed, they laid the

lovely little Bertha beside her mother; and Mary felt
that light had indeed almost gone out of life. Her
sorrow was more than she could bear. She tried to remember, that He does not willingly afflict the children
of men. She strove to look up to the God of her
mother, for help and comfort; and as she saw her
father's loneliness, she thought " Thou hast not left
me desolate;" and she prayed most earnestly, that
she might forget herself, that she might be all in all
to him—his hope, his joy, his pride, and his blessing.
And the whole love of her being centered in him, and
henceforth it was for him she studied, she read, she
the sigh of grief for the loss of mother and sister,
learned new music; in his presence she smothered
and with smiles was sometimes almost gay.

Yet a few months rolled along, and another misfortune burst suddenly upon Mr. Lincoln. He had very
largely indorsed for a business house, then thought
to be as safe as any in the country. It had failed,
and he found himself obliged to pay its liabilities.—
This sum took a large part of his capital, so that he
was obliged to sell his handsome dwelling, his pictures, carriages and horses, indeed, everything except
his plate, and a few household articles valued more
from association than for any other reason; and while
he took up his abode at a hotel, Mary was placed in
the family of Madame Robert, to whose school she
had been going for several years.

CHAPTER IV.

It was a great trial to Mary to give up all the comforts and luxuries to which she had always been accustomed. The privacy and quiet of her own pretty room were now exchanged for a great dormitory, whose innumerable beds each accommodated two young ladies: a dressing-room, where three or four wash-bowls sufficed for sixteen or eighteen persons, and each was obliged to wait her turn. The proverbial elegance of her father's table, and the quiet, tender tête-à-têtes with her mother, filled with good advice and instruction, which Mary so well remembered now, had given place to a boarding-school dining-room table, which, although presided over by a French woman, was arranged and provided by an Irish maid of all work, without order, without cleanliness, without taste.

Here, bad bread and unsavory butter ruled supreme; no luxuries came to grace the empty voids, for Madame Robert had no time to attend to housekeeping, and she had in vain tried to find a suitable person to fill the situation.

Some of her young ladies were unamiable enough to think, " where there's a will there's a way," and that it was madame's desire to make the most of her money, or rather to save it—which prevented a more comfortable state of affairs. But youth is not usually a fault-finding season—it is not often troubled with dyspepsia, and can sometimes eat bad bread and butter with a relish, particularly when it is accustomed to such diet.

So the pensionnaires whispered softly to each other about the fare, and after a time forgot it, especially as Madame Monin was not far away; and with plenty of money in their pockets, they were welcome visitors at her establishment, and were sure to be bountifully supplied with all they desired.

But Madame Robert was very kind, and they all loved her dearly. Learned, accomplished, elegant, and with most charming manners, she not only gained their esteem, but kept it forever. After the evening lessons were learned for the next day, at those times when Madame Robert denied herself to visitors, and gave herself up to her lady teachers and pupils, how delightful to hear her tell stories of her young days, when she went to school in beautiful Normandy; of her later travels—what wonderful things she had seen, what distinguished people she had met—and as her gentle voice dropped to almost a whisper in relating some of the incidents of her later life, so filled with losses, with sorrows, with reverses; and when inadvertently she spoke one evening of the death of her mother, sudden and fearful—her first grief—Mary Lincoln burst into an agony of sobs.

Mme Robert was frightened and pained at the sor-

row she had called forth; she folded the weeping girl
to her heart, and with many a caress asked pardon
for her seeming forgetfulness, while all the schoolmates pressed round with quiet tokens of sympathy.

Poor Mary Lincoln! It is the first time, in the
wide-awake presence of others, that she gives way to
her emotions of grief. But in the holy night, what
tears wet her pillow! In her holy dreams, does not
her mother, in the heavens, with angel face, stretch
forth her arms, and beckon to her to come upward,
where she is; and is not the prayer hourly in her
heart, "Oh, Father! upward, I beseech Thee; lead
me on and upward! Make me worthy to dwell there,
where Thine honor dwelleth, and where my mother
dwells!"

Henceforth, there was a bond of tenderness between teacher and scholar. Many were the sweet
smiles of approbation and love Madame Robert bestowed upon her favorite pupil. Much pains she
took to develop the intellect, and the taste of Mary's
really elegant mind.

And Mary, with the great pride and love of her
father strong in her being, made rapid advances.

"If my father can not bend down his great man's
heart to me, and take me up into it, he shall at least
respect me—he shall at least be proud of me," she
said; and with this thought uppermost, she worked,
she strove, she studied.

In these school-days, Mary seldom saw her father.
He was devoting every energy to the building up
again of his fortune; and between traveling here and

there, and the press of business, she rarely had a
visit from him.   But when he did come, he was very
kind, so attentive to her needs, so full of good counsel; for his responsibility in regard to his daughter
now weighed forcibly upon him, making him feel how
little unused he was to giving her good advice, to taking moral charge of her.

Mr. Lincoln was a little more demonstrative than
he had been, and every proof of his affection for his
daughter was hailed by her with joy, and treasured
up to carry with her through a life-time.

And nothing gave her so much happiness, as to
play and sing for her father, for he was very fond of
music.   What expression! what touch! she threw
into those intricate passages! what a delicate, exquisite sentiment in those admirable roulades! what pathos in the simple ballads, coming from and going to
the heart!   And when she saw her father's pleasure,
and heard his words of commendation, she would inwardly exclaim :

"Oh, music! I love thee, for my father loves thee;
and I will *serve* thee."

Hannah More says, in her strictures on female ed-
cation, that she can not help observing the common
fault of good people—the misappropriation of time.
One particular of this evil, is music.   Is there not
too much time literally wasted at the piano, which
might and ought to be spent in making acquisitions
that will furnish ideas to the head or useful employ-
ment to the hands?   Why should fashion usurp the
place of sense in this matter?   Why should not our

girls be taught those things which they will most need to know if they grow up to become wives and mothers, and heads of families? Let Christian parents consider well this important subject.

We do confess, that even in our day much time is consumed at the piano. Every young girl, love she music or not, is obliged to go through a course of musical instruction, in many cases as irksome as useless. But let us not ignore music entirely—banish it from all—because a very few learn the accomplishment to no purpose. It seems to me, that an hour's faithful practice of the piano, each day, instead of the "four hours at least," of which the author of Coelebs speaks, is quite sufficient to keep one of even ordinary musical talent, in good, in excellent practice. It seems to me, this acquisition gives more pleasure, more true delight to the generality of people than any other.— It elevates, it ennobles, it purifies, it sublimates a good mind. What a pleasure to the performer's friends! what a delight to the creator of this pleasure! I once remember to have heard a gifted friend say, "Of all my father has done for me, and you know how truly noble and generous he has always been—of all, there is nothing for which I thank him so much, as for my music. In joy, it has increased my happiness; in sorrow, it has solaced me; in loneliness, it has been my loved companion. My simple music has cheered many mourners: it has opened a world of delightful intercourse between strangers and myself: it has drawn to me kindred souls, and clasped the bond of love and friendship between us. There-

4

fore, every day of my life, I praise God for my music, and am more and more grateful to my father—and come cares, and trials, and heart-aches, and bodily pains, as long as I have strength to sit at the piano, or eyes to learn new music, I shall never, *never* give up my piano."

"Then, dear Mary Lincoln, go on with your music, and when your voice fails with age, rely on your fingers!"

CHAPTER V.

CHRISTMAS came and went—how unlike the last.— A few days before, Mary had received a purse of money from her father, nearly all of which she appropriated to buying presents for her teachers, and the domestics of the establishment.

On Christmas morning, Gertrude Clifford came to take Mary home with her for the holidays. Carrie Thomas and Kate Lee were to be of the party, and they were all to have a quiet time in the country, this rather dreary season. Mary (to speak truly) very much preferred quiet; for old thoughts and old memories would come stealing over her, in spite of herself, and the half-smothered sigh and the glistening tear-drop called up by association—at times well nigh mastered her. Not willing to obtrude her grief she made desperate efforts, and generally succeeded in being quite cheerful.

Mr. Clifford's country seat was about five miles from town. His elegant mansion with its bay windows, its wide marble halls and large porches stood in an inclosure of one hundred acres. On one side of the extensive lawn, groups of majestic trees reared their magnificent heads to the sky; small clumps of firs were scattered here and there in the distance, while trees, the shades of green of whose leaves contrasted well, were arranged together in admirable taste. Not very far from the foot of the lawn, rolled the beautiful river, and hill and dale diversified the country, adding much to the charm of the surrounding scenery.

Mr. Clifford, Gertrude's father, was a well kept, tall, handsome, well-proportioned, rosy-complexioned, silver-haired, genial old gentleman of sixty years.— His time having been at his own disposal, after finishing his collegiate course, he had spent many years abroad. He had not traveled for pastime, nor recreation alone; but had industriously stored up much valuable knowledge, not to be hidden away, selfishly concealed within his own soul, after the fashion of many who, having traveled in Europe, are ever afterward afraid to open their mouths, lest they may be called "snobbish," but to be brought to light, to be imparted freely, generously, fully, to all who ardently desired. Possessing fine descriptive talents, with a knowledge of the world, an insight into character, and a fund of humor, Mr. Clifford was a most charming companion, as well as a most courtly gentleman. His whole soul wrapped in Gertrude, his only child—his all—he lived for her alone. In vain feminine fascinations were paraded before him; in vain winning smiles endeavored to woo him, none were able to win him from his allegiance to his daughter.

And Gertrude repaid his love with all the devotion

of her whole heart. Her whole thought, her first and last prayer, her dreams by night and by day were of her cherished father. When her young friends remarked, "How very handsome your father is, Gertrude!" her eyes would light up more brightly, as she replied with a glad smile, "Isn't he the most splendid man you ever *did* see? My father is one of nature's noblemen." Gertrude often laughed and said, "Of all the grand women that ever lived, Madame de Stäel was the greatest, in my opinion; and sometimes I think I admire and worship her quite as much for her filial love, as I do for her genius—at least I think that in this respect we approach upon one level."

How cold this Christmas was in comparison with the last one! The lake at Clifford Place was skimmed over with ice; the trees were leafless, except the grand old firs, whose beauty Mary Lincoln thought was more observable in the dark winter time. The young girls had had a rapid and delightful ride, they said, in their warm wrappings within the old coach, as Mr. Clifford came out to meet them with his cordial greetings, and to help them to alight, and declared they had enjoyed the winter ride as much as in the balmiest spring day.

Gertrude immediately led the way up stairs, to the rooms assigned to her young friends. As the chambers communicated by large folding-doors, the girls expressed their pleasure at being all (as it were) in the same apartment; and Kate Lee declared they should have a cosy time of it.

Bright fires were blazing in both grates, and on the center-tables in each room stood bouquets of flowers. As her friends stooped over the flowers and inhaled their perfume, and like all young maidens went into ecstacies over their beauty, Gertrude remarked that these were all the Christmas present she should bestow on them to-day—that she had been puzzling herself what to get to make them the happiest, and had all at once concluded that flowers it should be.

"These, and a kiss, a kiss of welcome and affection," she said, as she advanced to bestow upon each the proffered embrace; "and if my gift be not grand, you will not deny, I am sure, that it is sentimental—and sweet, too, is it not?"

"Very sweet, I ween, is the second part of our appropriate and charming gift," said Kate Lee; "and very highly prized the same will be two or three years hence, by some favored swain."

"Oh, Kate, my darling! let us banish all [such disagreeable subjects to-day," replied Gertrude, as she busied herself, stowing away mantles, bonnets, and furs.

Hair smoothed, and the folds of dresses arranged, all four young ladies took their way downward to the bright drawing-room, where no one awaited them, Mr. Clifford having gone out to superintend some laborers.

Cheerful fires burned in the shining grates, and here too, beautiful flowers lent their fragrance to the genial atmosphere of the room.

Soon, three young heads bent charmed over a crystal dish of lovely rose-buds, while Gertrude stood at a little distance, smilingly noting their exclamations of admiration.

"Why, Gertrude," said Kate Lee, "where *did* you get such exquisite rose-buds at this time of year?—surely you did not raise them yourself?"

"No," said Gertrude, shaking her head.

"Did a more perfect bud ever grow, than this lovely Adam tea, so large, so rich in color, so deliciously fragrant?" said Carrie Thomas.

"And look at this beautiful straw-colored, half-opened rose, nestling so timidly in among these magnificent white Lamarques!" said Mary Lincoln.

"I never *did* see such perfect buds," said all.

"And let me tell you, cara mia," said Kate Lee, turning to Gertrude, "*somebody* has arranged them with much taste. See how this purple heliotrope is blended in and around the other delicate colors! and now tell us, if you please, where these paragons of beauty came from?"

And they all drew up their chairs and sat down, Gertrude in the midst.

"Well, listen my friends, and I will my short rosy story relate," said Gertrude. "You have all, without doubt, heard of Feffinger's green-house?"

"Yes, yes!" was the reply.

"Well, on yesterday afternoon, full of the delightful idea of finding some choice flowers with which to greet my best friends on their arrival," bowing to her companions, "I ordered out the barouche, provided myself with a good-sized basket, put on my bonnet and furs, as the day was rather cold, you know, and stepping into the carriage, I told Jack to drive to the neighborhood of Feffinger's green-houses, imagining I could easily find the place from the directions I had already received. In the course of half an hour, without accident, and without adventure, we found ourselves, as I supposed, approaching Feffinger's. I ordered Jack to stop—I alighted with dignity."

"No need of such extremely minute particulars, mon amie," said Carrie Thomas.

Gertrude smiled, and continued:

"I took my basket on my arm; I walked up the short avenue leading to the glass-houses, stopping a moment to admire a magnificent group of pine trees; I raised the latch of the green-house; I opened the door, and there, standing at a little distance before me, was—a—pleasant, intelligent, gentlemanly-looking man—don't raise your expectations too high, thinking I am going off into a wonderful little romance—a middle-aged man, and père de famille, I doubt not.

"I bowed and asked if this was Feffinger's.

"He bowed, and said no—that the place I was seeking was about a quarter of a mile away. I raised my eyes, and seeing an immense rose-bush whose drooping buds hung in lovely profusion over my head, forthwith I went into alarming ecstacies at the view. As soon as reason returned, I said, 'Since I am here, sir, will you allow me to look at your flowers?' He looked pleased, and said, ' With the greatest pleasure, miss; and if you admire *that* rose-bush so much, I can show you one vastly its superior.' So saying, he led me through two or three different green-houses, filled with blooming plants, when, suddenly turning to the left, we entered one devoted to a single rose-bush. What do you think of that, young ladies?— One single rose-bush, covered with clusters of these lovely white buds you see before you, and filling one entire side, and part of another, of a green-house fifty feet long! I do not exaggerate, as I shall take you to-morrow to the same place, if you would like to go, and you may judge and measure the stem of the bush, and count, if you can, the number of buds on one cluster. Oh! the pure lovely beauty of those delicious roses! I clasped my hands and exclaimed, in unmeasured, heartfelt words of admiration, which so pleased my cicerone that he politely requested me to come again, and bring as many friends as I chose, to see his treasure, which will have arrived at perfection in two or three days. I have not been so happy for a long time as I was, when, with my precious burden on my arm, I jumped into the vehicle to return home, scarcely daring, through fear of the frost, to peep at my beauties—but longing even for the sympathy of Jack on this occasion. It is needless to say," continued Gertrude, " that papa was as much delighted with my purchase as I was—and here he comes to testify to what I have just said, that you were quite as enthusiastic about my roses as I was— n'est ce pas, mon cher papa?" continued Gertrude, as

5

she rose (her young companions making way for her), and placed a chair for her father.

Mr. Clifford bent such a look of fondness on his daughter, as sent a pang to the heart of Mary Lincoln, and she thought,

"Oh! the world for one such look from my father on me!"

Julie opened the door and announced dinner.

CHAPTER VI.

AFTER tea, Gertrude asked Mary to play upon the piano, which request was so warmly seconded by Mr. Clifford and the young ladies present, that Mary rose immediately, and saying, "I can not play much without music—but I think you have some of my pieces here, Gertrude," seated herself at the piano, took up one of Beethoven's sonatos, and, while her auditors listened profoundly silent, played, as she always played, like one inspired. When she had finished, Mr. Clifford led her from the piano, thanked her for the pleasure she had given, seated her beside him on the sofa, and said in a low tone:

"My daughter, votre musique, quelle consolation pour vous!"

Mary felt in the inmost depths of her heart this quiet word of sympathy, and was grateful.

At this moment, the door opened to admit Mr. and Mrs. Day, neighbors of Mr. Clifford, and long time friends.

Mary had often heard her mother speak of Mrs. Day as a friend and associate, but had never seen her, as she had been absent with her husband a number of years in Europe, and had only returned last summer.

When they were introduced, Mrs. Day did not hear Mary's name, but after a moment or two she said:

"While we stood at your door, Mr. Clifford, we heard the last strains of delicious music; will whoever was playing be so kind as to repeat the piece for my especial benefit?"

"Mary, will you play again?" asked Mr. Clifford.

Mary blushed slightly, looked at Mrs. Day, and in a low sweet tone replied:

"With pleasure, sir."

Mr. Clifford seated her at the piano, arranged her music, and resumed his former place.

Mary played again the same sonata. When she had finished, and as she rose, Mrs. Day said to Gertrude:

"What is your young guest's name, that I may thank her?"

Gertrude again presented Mary to Mrs. Day, who soon discovered her to be the daughter of her former friend, and said to her:

"How charmingly you play, Mary! Your music carried me to heaven. I soared far away above the clouds on those beautiful notes, and caught glimpses of the angels. That divine music of Beethoven!— those harmonious chords, filling the soul with melody! How much more grand such music, than the style so much in vogue at present! These simple airs, covered with a frost-work of notes, through which you can scarcely discern the original, I must confess, I do not like. Give me instead, the rich, solemn, massive style! Do you not agree with me, Mr. Clifford?"

"I do not know," said Mr. Clifford, "that I am a *judge* of music. I hope, Mrs. Day, you will not think me devoid of taste, when I say, that although I believe I appreciate and enjoy the kind of music of which you have just spoken, particularly the minor passages, yet I *do* like those simple melodies which steal out upon me from underneath their glittering net-work. 'The Dew-drops of Morning,' 'The Songs of Spring,' 'The Carol of Birds,' 'The Wandering Streamlet,' and others of this class, transport me in fancy to green meadows, bring before me silent valleys, silver streams, murmuring rivulets, and make me feel again all the freshness and all the buoyancy of youth."

"Mary, please play for Mrs. Day, Thalberg's Sweet Home," said Mr. Clifford, turning to Mary.— "It is a contrast to the sonata you have given us, but in its style is, to my thinking, quite as impressive."

With her usual grace and simplicity of manner, Mary sat down to perform the "Sweet Home," giving to every note in the rich melody its pathos, its touching sadness, thrilling with tenderness the hearts of her hearers, and afterward carrying the strain, with clearness, with accent, with taste, through the intricate variations.

As Mary finished, Mrs. Day, who had risen from her seat and was standing beside her, said:

"Thank you again and again for the pleasure you

have given me. Believe me, my dear, you have a rare taste for music."

Mary, in a low voice, replied :

" It creates much of my happiness."

How pleasantly the remainder of the evening passed in that elegant country home, enriched by the hand of genius, adorned by the wealth of elegant tastes, graced by the presence of intellect and minds in a constant state of progress and cultivation.

As Mr. Day and Mr. Clifford, deep in the discussion of horticultural and agricultural questions, touched upon the different component parts of earth, the mixing of soils, the varieties of fruit, the planting and culture of trees, the last new roses, their habits, then spoke of the superb roses seen abroad ; and glanced from them to the emperor of France, to the great changes and improvements going on in Paris under his supervision; and from this to their travels, to their tour in Germany, to their visit to Italy, to the pictures, sculpture specialities seen— Mary listened, absorbed, and thought, " how refresh-ing such social hours ! How cheering, how enliven-ing—how they prepare one for the duties, and even for the battles of life !"

Mr. and Mrs. Day, in bidding them good-night, in-vited them all to tea the next evening, and insisted upon their coming early—sans ceremonie.

Mr. Clifford stroked back his daughter's wavy hair, and with a holy kiss, and a " God bless you, my darling !" he bade her and her friends " good night."

After he had gone, the young quartette lingered

over the fire, asking questions of Gertrude about Mrs. Day.

"I can not tell you much of Mrs. Day," said Gertrude, "except that she is an old resident in the neighborhood, although with Mr. Day she has often been absent. Her husband is twice her age, and adores her, and for a wonder, is pleased that others should regard his charming wife with pretty much the same feeling—and she idolizes him."

"Perhaps that's the secret of his adoration!" chimed in Kate Lee.

"In short, they are supremely happy—or would be so, if they had sons and daughters. Mrs. Day, twelve years ago, lost her only child, a girl, five years old. She grieves still profoundly for her daughter, and the sad, almost mournful, expression which sometimes steals over her countenance, even in the midst of a smile, reveals the still sorrowing heart. Although I am young, yet when we are alone together, she often, with tears in her eye, speaks to me of her lost child, and my sympathy seems a solace to her. Mr. Day's kindness and attention to his wife are remarkable."

"How young she looks to have been married so long!" said Kate Lee.

"And how beautiful she is, with those magnificent, soft, black eyes, and those drooping eyelashes—those are *wonderful* eyelashes!" said Carrie Thomas.

"And did you ever see such hair!" said Gertrude, "and such a clear, transparent complexion?"

"And teeth so beautiful, so white!" said Kate Lee.

"And what have you to say, Mary dear?" asked

Gertrude; " will you not join us in our admiration of
Mrs. Day?"

" You have all said so much," smiled Mary, " that
there is little left for me, except (and which in the
opinion of many is of equal if not more importance),
her manners are very lady-like; her figure is very
graceful and elegant; her conversation is refined and
dignified."

" What more can we add," said Gertrude, " to finish the picture of my dear Mrs. Day, except, and the
best of all yet is, that she is a Christian, and truly
one of those women of whom the Psalmist says, ' Her
price is far above rubies.' "

" And now," said Gertrude, looking at the clock
on the mantelpiece, " my dear children, it is quite
time we were all in bed. We are country people,
you know, and think it a dreadful thing to sit up
after eleven o'clock at night."

" You are surely joking," said Kate Lee, in a de-
mure way, as they wended quietly up to the great
rooms above.

CHAPTER VII.

MARY LINCOLN was restless and could not sleep.—
The moon shone in at the window; the night was
lovely, and Mary thought (her companion breathed
so softly and regularly in her placid sleep) that she
would get up stealthily, not disturbing her, and look
out over the wintry landscape.

The night was superb, and Mary wandered in silent
enjoyment from one window to another.

On the right of the house, the full moon sailing in
all its majesty in the cloudless heavens, just skirted
the intertwining boughs of a group of towering oak
trees. The broad lawn, part in shadow and part in
full light, swept off to the gleaming fences in the distance, and the porter's lodge, far to the left, peered
out from behind its screen of fir-trees. Across the
white road, the shadows of leafless trees fell in pen-
ciled beauty. A half mile away, almost at the back
of Mr. Clifford's place, some lights still shone out
through the pretty village windows, while nearer to
the right, a short distance off, Mary could discern the
tower of Mr. Day's dwelling.

With a glowing heart she wandered from one window to another, taking in different views of the same

scene. She was surprised that she had never before observed the exquisite grace and beauty of a leafless tree; and as she gazed at the different shapes and varieties, at the hills and vales, the far-off river, the blue heavens and the silvery moon, her heart involuntarily lifted itself up to God, and she said:

"For these, O Father! the work of Thy hands, may we adore thee. In Thy love, which gives us all and exacts so little, may we rejoice! Fill us with an ever-growing admiration of Nature; with gratitude for the tastes Thou hast implanted in the heart of man; with an ever-increasing love for Thee—a love which lives in THEE, and in THEE moves, and in THEE has its being."

And then, a moment after, looking out again, those words of Victor Hugo she had lately read, passed through her mind, and she realized that she was just feeling to the utmost the truth he has so vividly expressed, that the contemplation of Nature fills its admirers "with hope, with love, with prayer, and ecstasy."

But a quick word from her room-mate roused her and set her trembling for a moment, suddenly dispelling her thoughts.

"Good gracious, Mary Lincoln! what in this world are you doing wandering about like a ghost this cold night? You'll certainly be sick to-morrow. What *are* you doing?"

"Nothing, except looking at the trees; and oh! Katie, dear, do just get up one moment and see what a grand night this is. Who would have thought the

trees so beautiful without their leaves! I never imagined it before," said Mary.

"You silly girl!" responded Kate; "do you think
I am going to get out of a warm bed to look at a few
dreary trees, and catch a chill which might last me a
month? Do come to bed and go to sleep. If you
don't have a care, I'll complain to-morrow of somnambulists, and petition for a change of bed-fel-
lows."

The next morning, as Mary caught the merry
glance of Kate, at the breakfast table, she very much
feared her companion would tell tales of her, but
Kate behaved unusually well, and was more silent
than Mary had expected.

The friends planned their arrangements for the
day; a walk, and a visit to Feffinger's rose-buds, and
Mr. Clifford bade them good morning, telling them
not to tire themselves too much, but to remember
they had promised this evening to Mrs. Day.

The hours passed rapidly and delightfully, and
evening came, finding them in a sort of trepidation
at the idea of visiting a stranger. Mary could scarcely
analyze her feelings; she desired at least an interest
in Mrs. Day's thoughts; she had even a yearning for
more than an acquaintance. She had an intense sympathy, a deep admiration for this lady, a stranger to
her, but known long and highly valued by her mother.
And in Mrs. Day's heart she had awakened equal
warmth.

Has any one defined—can any one explain this inexplicable sentiment, this similarity between persons, of thought, of feeling, of tastes, of pursuits—this blending as it were of two minds into one? What is it that draws us with strong chords toward some and repels us from others? I have met some people day after day during years—I have been associated intimately with them—I have very often walked with them, and talked friendlily with them—at the end of a long period I have found it was utterly impossible they should understand me, and I could not comprehend them. Again—I have seen others, who seemed at the first instant of meeting to strike a chord which always in after years reverberated—those for whom admiration and love started to life at once—they whose companionship ever after gave me the most intense delight. I recall here those words of Frederika Bremer:

" There are eternal harmonies, eternal sympathies; people are found who were born united. When they meet each other in life—then the bond of friendship is quickly tied, then arises that mutual attraction toward each other, that inward sympathy between two beings which the finite understanding can not explain—which it is not now the fashion to believe in, but which is found nevertheless and felt with pure delight in those hearts where it manifests itself. They are sparks springing up from mysteries which may well be called Elysian."

Blissful mysteries, indeed! rendering life, otherwise cold, dead, cheerless—warm, rich and blessed.

Mary dressed herself with more care than usual

(she was yet in deep black), and sighed as she looked in the mirror, and then at Gertrude, at Kate and at Carrie, in all their maiden loveliness, that she was not more like them. She fancied her tribute of love would be more acceptable to Mrs. Day, perhaps her presence more highly prized were she beautiful. The thought that her youth (when contrasted with the budding and blossoming charms of her companions) might perhaps be an excuse—solaced her.

When they arrived at Mr. Day's residence, which had been newly modeled and fitted up during the absence of the family, and which struck Mary as very modern and graceful, the door was opened by a tall, pretty, aristocratic looking young person, in black with a small white linen collar, and a dainty white cambric apron. This was Margeurite, Mrs. Day's graceful French girl, admired, esteemed, and beloved by her mistress, which sentiments she returned with an increasing devotion.

As they entered the immense drawing-room, Mrs. Day rose from her low arm-chair, and came forward, greeting them all with cordiality, and Mary with a look of interest, very plainly revealing it was not the first time she had thought of her since last evening. After they were all seated, Mary stole a glance at Mrs. Day, and thought how lovely she looked in her rich black velvet dress, her tiny lace collar and elegant lace undersleeves. Her magnificent black hair was braided and twisted into a large knot on the back of her head, while the bandeaux in front (Mary thought them almost too glossy and smooth) were drawn tightly over her ears, showing only the lower part of this pretty feature, and the beautiful diamond pendants, which she always wore. A small diamond cross fastened her collar. Her complexion was so fresh, so pure, the expression of her face so tranquil and to-night so smiling, that Mary thought, "here is a mind at peace with all the world; here is a favored one of Fortune; God grant her prosperity always!"

At the end of the almost regal drawing-room, in a large bay window, almost hidden by the purple velvet and lace folds of the curtains, stood a statue Mr. Day had bought in Italy, which had arrived but a few days before.

Mrs. Day advanced, and drawing aside the curtains, desired Mr. Clifford to express his opinion as to its merits. All rose to look at it.

It was a Scripture piece; the subject, the three Marys at the tomb of Christ.

For some minutes, not a word was spoken, while all gazed with different emotions, and Mr. Clifford viewed it with the eye of a connoisseur, walking round and round it, and moving the pedestal so as to get the best light upon it. One of the three figures was kneeling, the other two standing. Mary particularly observed the central figure of the group, the Mary Magdalene, whose graceful attitude, whose lovely expression of countenance, whose breast she almost thought was heaving with its weight of sorrow, so touched her to pity, to divine love, that spite of herself two great tears came stealing down her cheeks.

To suppress her feelings, she walked quickly and silently away to the other side of the room, where hung a picture which she had noticed on entering, but not before her hostess had observed her wiping stealthily away the tear-drops; she again approached the group, who were intent upon the statue, and said to Mrs. Day who came and stood beside her,

" How much they loved Him !"

On the great marble table, at one side of the fireplace, lay immense volumes, engravings of ancient Rome. The young girls found much in these to interest and gratify them, and had a fine opportunity of displaying their historical knowledge.

Now Margeurite came in and said tea was ready, and Mrs. Day put her arm tenderly around Mary, as if to claim her for herself, and asked them all to walk into the dining-room. How bright and cheerful glowed this room, with its warm crimson velvet carpet, its crimson curtains, its massive side-board laden with crystal and silver !

They sat down to a "country supper," Mrs. Day said—oyster and chicken-salad, with hot coffee and chocolate.

Mary thought it a very hospitable meal, and carried her back to her own dear, lost home. Mr. Clifford, approved of such suppers, when people dined at one or two o'clock, as they usually did in these environs, but at the same time mentioned his astonishment when he first came to the West, to see tea-tables laden with meats of many varieties, so differ-

ent a custom from that followed at the North and
East.

Margeurite, in her pretty white cap and apron,
glided noiselessly about the table, anticipating every
one's wants, and seemed to do everything by magic.

After tea, Mrs. Day showed her guests her cabinet
of curiosities, of specialities; filagree work from
Genoa, glass from Vienna, garnets from Frankfort,
cameos, beads, coral, furs, silks, music box, and many
wonderful little things from the Palais Royal, all interesting, particularly to school girls.

Gertrude asked if she objected to showing her laces,
Mrs. Day replied, certainly not, and rang the bell,
and sent Margeurite to bring them, and told her to
bring the Geneva pin also. Mary was not much of a
judge of laces, but the other young ladies went into
such raptures over this display, that Many quite
laughed at their enthusiasm.

The pin was exquisitely beautiful, and such an one,
that all might delight to possess. It was a large flat
garnet, set in Etruscan, and in the center a fly of diamond, which sparkled brilliantly on the dark, rich,
transparent back ground.

Mrs. Day regretted she had no piano, for she was
longing for instrumental music to-night, but as there
was a guitar in the room, and in good order, she said,
perhaps there might be some one among so many
charming young ladies, who could sing.

"And to set a good example," she said, "I will
commence with one of my simple songs, hoping you
will *all* perhaps follow."

Mr. Day sprang for the guitar, which he handed to his wife, who took it with a beaming smile for him, tuned it up a little, and sang a sweet song "divinely."

Mary could not but observe how admiringly Mr. Day gazed at his wife, and when she had finished, how politely he added his thanks to those of her other hearers.

Gertrude now sang, and then all eyes were turned to Mary, who received the instrument and, unexpectedly (for no one present had ever heard her sing), drew her fingers over the chords and commenced a sweet plaintive melody, which made the hearts of all tremble with a sort of melancholy thrill. After she had played the last symphony, Kate Lee exclaimed,

"Oh Mary, your music goes through and through me, like a cold chill; my hair surely stands on end, does n't it?" and drawing close to Mary, she continued: "Do look, Mary! If Dickens were here to-night, his doubts on this subject would be put to rest, for he would become aware of the fact that people's hair *does* sometimes bristle up, the effect of their emotions."

"Take care, Kate," laughed Gertrude, "that you hear no more songs of our dear little Mary Lincoln, or your hair might grow 'white in a single night,' 'as men's have done with sudden fears.'"

"Oh!" said Kate, "I do not anticipate such a shocking calamity, but for fear of her power over me,

7

or her music's power, I think it would be well to keep
out of her presence, don't you, Gertrude ?"

Mary blushed, and thought of somnambulists, and
dreaded the merry Kate's tongue; but Mrs. Day
smiled kindly and said : ·

"My dear Miss Lee, I am sure our young friend
will exert for *good* only, the powers God has given
her."

"Since my song has had such an unpleasant effect,
dear Katie," said Mary, "and has produced disagreeable anticipations, let me hasten to remove its impression, and sing something which, I am sure, you will
like better."

Then such a gush of melody, harmonious, clear,
sweet and bird-like came from those pure young lips,
as caused all to hold their breath in delight.

"Her music is wonderful," said Mrs. Day, in a low
tone to Mr. Clifford; "what a lovely and charming
girl she is, too—and, heaven pity her! she is motherless! What would I give for such a daughter ?"

"Yes," said Mr. Clifford, "she is indeed good and
lovely ! "

And then turning to Mary, he thanked her, in the
name of all, for her sweet songs, and wished her to
feel that, although the first song differed very much
from the last, it had given in reality quite as much
pleasure.

At parting, Mrs. Day put both arms round Mary,
kissed her affectionately, and hoped Madame Robert
would allow her to spend at least part of her next
holidays with her.

Mary, grateful for Mrs. Day's kindness, went back to Mr. Clifford's with a heart full of joy. The pleasant week, fairly *flew* away, and Mary returned to school again cheerful and most grateful to God for friendship.

CHAPTER VIII.

MADAME ROBERT received Mary with much affection, and complimented her upon her improved looks, and thought she ought to go often to the country, change of air seemed so beneficial to her. With renewed strength and enjoyment, Mary again took up her books, determined to progress rapidly.

A few months wore away monotonously, but still in the performance of pleasant duties, varied only by several visits from Mrs. Day, and by the reception from her of most lovely flowers, which Mary tended and put in cool water many times a day, the better to preserve their freshness, and which lasted a wonderful length of time (her schoolmates said) owing to her devotion. These species of flowers were ever afterward, in Mary's sight, filled with visions of the graceful Mrs. Day, in her rich, grave dresses, her beautiful laces, her shining bands of soft black hair, and the sweet, sad smile on her lovely face.

Mary saw her father every week; he said he was tired of living at hotels, and he should build himself a house, and Mary must try her skill at housekeeping. Mary's heart beat quickly at the idea of having again a home; and although she loved Madame Robert dearly, she often sighed for the quiet and the comfort of her father's house.

One evening, early in May, Mr. Lincoln came to pay his daughter a farewell visit. He said, he was going far away the next day, to be absent several weeks, and he told Mary to write him often, and to direct her letters to Boston, from which place they would be forwarded to him.

Mary thought her father's farewell was more tender than it had ever been ; he even turned back twice and kissed and embraced her, as if for the last time. After he had gone, a gloom like a pall came over her ; she felt more than ever alone—*Oh! alone!* in the world. Was it a presentiment of evil, Mary Lincoln ? was this the last time your father should ever kiss you with a kiss of warm affection ? henceforward were you and he to be strangers to each other, unknown and misunderstood ?—the father you loved with your entire devotion ; the father for whom you lived, to whom your intellect, your tastes, your every thought was offered up, in secret adoration yearning intensely for a look, a smile from him, as your great reward? Yes! from this day henceforward you are scarcely nothing in his sight ; your longings will be met by him with coldness ; your best motives, misconstrued ; your best actions, misinterpreted ; your signs of tenderness and love, mayhap, repulsed! Heaven pity you, poor child, in your sorrow, in your agony, and make you strong to bear—meek, to endure the years that await you!

Every week Mary received a letter from her father ; kind, very kind letters, filled with good advice, and

pleasant descriptions of travel, and new acquaintances.
One day there came a missive marked "confidential."
She hastened to her room, in trepidation broke the
seal, and read—the news—of his approaching union
with a New England lady. He did not wish this
made known—at least, until after the consummation
of the marriage, which would take place immediately,
and so bound Mary to secresy. He said he had met,
had traveled with this lovely woman, so elegant, so
superior, so fitted to be the mother of his child, and
he hoped Mary would render to her all the admiration
and affection due.

As for the admiration, thought Mary, I have no
doubt, if she is such a woman as my father describes
her, it may be due from me; but for the affection,
that is quite a different affair. How can my father
expect me to love, unless I am first loved, a person
I never saw—I never before heard of—especially
when such a one comes to take the place of my dear
dead mother ?

Mary burst into an agony of tears, and was supremely wretched. She threw herself on the solitary
bed of the small chamber Madame Robert had recently
given her, sobbed, and sobbed again in the pillows.
She rose and locked her door and paced the floor of
her room almost in a convulsion of tears.

Miss Flavian came to call her to a recitation, but
without turning her key she said, in a trembling
voice, that her head ached severely, and she must be
excused.

An hour passed in this way, Mary thinking, " Oh

my father, my dear father is lost to me—perhaps my
new mother will hate me—perhaps she will not let me
live at home at all—perhaps I shall be sent desolate
away among strangers." Doleful visions of the future
floated before Mary's aching brain, and with each
thought she sobbed and sobbed again.

Madame Robert now came and knocked at Mary's
door for admittance. She started, when she saw these
evidences of grief, and divined the cause of all—the
open letter on the floor. Her delicacy was too great
to ask questions—she only sympathized with her dear
pupil in her suffering of body—she asked her only if
she could do nothing for her headache—she folded
her in her arms—she laid her head on her bosom—
she smoothed back her disordered hair, and hoped she
would soon be better. Madame Robert was quite
prepared for the reception, a few days after, of the
news of the marriage of Mr. Lincoln, and still later,
for the arrival of himself and his new wife.

CHAPTER IX.

I⊤ was a bright, lovely morning in June, when Mr.
Lincoln came to take Mary with him to the hotel, to
call on her new mother. He had reached home
early this morning, and hastened immediately after
breakfast to see his daughter and to accompany
her to pay her respects to one in whose keeping
her happiness was now to be placed. With a flushed
cheek and a proud stifling of all appearance of emotion, Mary walked quietly beside her father, through
the crowded streets, not far to the hotel where Mr.
Lincoln had taken up his residence until the completion of his house. Mary was yet in deep mourn-
ing. Her father had forgotten to tell her to lay it
aside, so that, after Mary's introduction, he was
obliged to apologize to his new wife for this seeming
disrespect, and to desire her, if not too much fatigued,
to accompany Mary to purchase a new outfit of colored
garments. As Mary had leave of absence from school
this week, Mrs. Lincoln cordially assented to her
husband's proposition, saying that, as she was in perfect health, she did not feel in the least fatigued.

While Mrs. Lincoln was making her preparations to go with Mary, Mary had an opportunity of scanning her new mother and coming to some conclusions in regard to her. The first was, that she was rather pretty, or fine-looking. She was not very tall, medium-sized, with a full, round figure, rather embonpoint, clear complexion, large blue eyes, broad forehead, and very beautiful curls of dark-brown hair. A small tuck-comb of silver confined her back hair, from which a few straggling ringlets floated in graceful confusion. She was quite as old, Mary thought, as her father; perhaps a year or two older. There was something of energy even in the manner in which she tied her bonnet, and care for appearance in the last twist she gave her coquettish curls.

Mr. Lincoln handed a well-filled purse to Mrs. Lincoln, as he parted from her and his daughter at the steps of the hotel, and remarked, he would meet them at dinner.

Mary soon discovered her mother's first virtue—economy. In the purchase of summer fabrics for an entire new trousseau, she planned, and arranged, and decided how many were necessary; at least, she told Mary how much better it was to have a small number only—as few as were absolutely indispensable—"for," said she, "while you are growing, Mary, it is not advisable to have many dresses, as they may be useless to you another year; and beside, you know, the fashion changes so often! and it is better to content ourselves with material not too fine or too costly, for

7

your father tells me that, within the last year or two, his fortunes are quite altered."

Mary knew that her father was not so rich as he had been; but she had never been stinted in regard to her wants, especially her clothing, and the thought of being scrimped, was new to her, and not at all amusing. After the purchases were made, Mary was about ordering them to her mantua-maker, but Mrs. Lincoln said, "No! we will make the dresses at home."

Mary remarked, with a sort of protest in her voice, that she had never done such a thing in her life, and that she had no time to make garments, and but little time to keep in order those she had, when Mrs. Lincoln said:

"You are quite old enough to learn, Mary, and must endeavor to *find* time. I will cut and fit the dresses for you, and will show you how to sew them."

Mary did not feel more than usually cheerful, on their way to the hotel. She was obliged to sit down, immediately after dinner, prepared with thimble, thread and needle, to run up the breadths of a dress which Mrs. Lincoln had torn from the stuff, while the latter drew from her trunk the last fashion-plate, soliciting Mary's attention as to the style she preferred.

Mr. Lincoln sat by, reading, but every now and then cast a glance of satisfaction and of admiration at his new wife.

Mary was kept faithfully and unrelentingly at work, from morning till night, during the remainder of the week, and felt a great burden of ennui and fatigue

roll away, when the time came for her to return to
Madame Robert.   Mrs. Lincoln did not fail to observe
the relief Mary's countenance expressed, when she
came to bid her good-by, and her impression of dislike
to the silent, timid girl, was in a measure heightened.
She had married Mr. Lincoln with the resolve to do
her duty by his daughter; her whole duty, in every
respect; that is, according to her own ideas, and,
being a Christian, she had already offered up many
prayers for the fulfillment of her purpose.   If she
had mistaken ideas of duty, and was too hard and too
strict with her young charge; if she ignored love,
affection, kind words of encouragement, of sympathy, of praise; if she devoted Mary to the stern
necessities totally excluding in her creed all the
pleasures, all the agrèmens of life, let us not blame
her too harshly.   Her own education was to serve as
a model for that of Mary; and having, for the greater
part of her life, lived among snow, and ice, and rocks,
she had gathered from this cold atmosphere a hard
and icy theory.   If she had met the poor, shrinking
child with a kiss, expressive at least of interest, instead of the half-given, half-reluctant embrace it was;
if she had put her arms around Mary, and had said,
"Dear child, I have come to be your mother, and pray
God we may love each other tenderly," then the heart
of the young girl, longing for affection, would have
unfolded itself to this other heart, would have rejoiced in all the wealth of this long-desired, attained
wish, and would have been hers forever.   If she had
even devoted the first few days of her acquaintance

with this hitherto tenderly-nurtured girl, to a little
recreation of body or soul, and not eternally sung,
"duty, duty," it would have been happier, happier
always, for both stepmother and daughter.

Mary's summer holidays were spent with Madame
Robert, varied by a delightful visit of two weeks to
Gertrude Clifford and Mrs. Day.   The neighborhood,
in that region, was rapidly increasing—filling up with
agreeable families, and Mary accompanied Mrs. Day
and Gertrude several times, in their calls upon the
new comers.

Mrs. Day and Gertrude had called upon Mrs. Lin
coln immediately upon her arrival; and the admiration on both sides was mutual.   Mrs. Lincoln was
decidedly a brilliant woman—a person who had seen
much of the world; who had mingled in the most cultivated society of New England—had spent much of
her time in the Athens of America, and was proud to
claim relationship with many of the distinguished men
of her country.   She excelled in the charms of conversation.   Her rounded sentences, flowing, harmonious and elegant, betrayed a spirit not only accustomed to think deeply upon all subjects which
interested her; to weigh, to reason, to investigate for
itself, but also a natural grace, which she had assiduously cultivated.

Her ready mind seemed to grasp, to comprehend,
to be familiar with every topic brought under discussion; and phrases replete with new ideas, fascinating
by her own peculiar individuality, fell from her lips

like so many jewels. She even condescended, at
times, to be "refreshingly nonsensical," but none
the less charming. Mrs. Lincoln never threw down
great massive rocks of sarcasm, of envy, of bitter-
ness—stumbling rocks of offense to her listeners; she
scattered in their pathway exquisite roses, which they
delighted to stoop, to gather, to place in their bosoms,
and whose delicious fragrance seemed to call forth
new life from their souls—to unseal the fountains of
youth — to bring forth hidden treasures from the
caverns of memory. What a light is such an one in
the social circle! What a murmur of disappointment
goes round should their presence be denied! How
we watch and wait, all silently, their coming; and
when their musical footfall is at last heard, and the
rustling of their garments betokens their approach,
how every eye glistens with anticipated delight—how
every languid form raises itself to its full height,
warmed into new being by this " star round which its
thoughts revolve like satellites."

Mr. Lincoln hung upon his wife's words like one
enchanted, and soon, to him, her slightest will was
law. Assured, in his own mind, of her wisdom, her
good sense, he consulted her in his most important,
as well as his minor business affairs. Her judgment,
in this short period of their married life, had never
failed to select the road prosperity traveled.

Mrs. Lincoln esteemed and admired her husband;
his noble qualities she thought unsurpassed; and she
was determined he should bow at her shrine now and
always—no love should ever come between him and

her—she would be first and foremost, as every wife
ought to be in the heart of her husband. With
this end in view, she continued to be self-provident;
she had never fought the battle of life; she had never
known want, or the cares, and burdens, and woe of
most women's days; free to come and go when she
pleased, to pass her hours as best suited her, naturally
always sitting in the warm sunshine of life, her soul
and her body were in the flush of youth and of health;
and thus she intended to keep them. For her husband's eyes, then, the beautiful complexion was
shielded from scorching rays and winds, the silken
curls were carefully arranged, the fine figure was
always kept trim, the simple, pretty morning-dress
and snow-white collar were donned, and then always
changed before dinner for her fresh, pure, afternoon
costume; for him her face was wreathed in smiles;
her pretty little work-basket was brought out, and her
chair and her stool were placed close beside him,
while his full, male voice read to her pieces of her
own selection.

Mr. Lincoln now found much more time at his own
disposal than a year or two ago he would have imagined possible. Happy in the unspoken marks of esteem and preference his wife so delicately paid him,
he was unconsciously becoming a different man. He
never failed to compliment her upon her style of dress,
her choice of pattern, its becoming shade, the neatness of her slipper, the beauty of the gauze-like stock-
ing, to say nothing of the little foot which nestled so
lovingly in the soft cushion at his side.

Oh! if men knew how gratifying it is to a wife to be noticed occasionally by her husband, to be praised, to be encouraged in her weary monotonous routine of life, would not more hearts be gladdened, strengthened to renew with vigor their innumerable duties. How much might the domestic hearth be brightened, by these little gallantries which cost nothing, but which are so precious, so dear! May not this husbandly inattention, this neglect, at first the cause of many a pang to the loving wife, afterward become the source of indifference, perhaps at last of dislike?

Are there not some for whom the rose-colored hues of early married life, fade away all too soon, and who wake rudely to the knowledge that slight causes at first, becoming more and more insupportable, are banishing gradually her love for the man of her choice, that love which she believed ever-enduring, ever immortal, and with a low wail of misery, she lays her head and her heart in the dust, as this light, this joy of her existence takes forever its flight!

Both Mrs. Day and Gertrude were quite charmed with Mary's new mother, and did not fail to express their opinion to Mary, to whom also Mrs. Lincoln spoke in unmeasured terms of admiration, of the grace and lady-like dignity of Mrs. Day, and the sweet simplicity, self-possession and beauty of her friend Gertrude. Mary was happy in hearing two persons, of whom she thought so highly, so commended, and fully agreed with her friends in the sentence their taste and judgment passed upon the genial and captivating manners of her mother.

The fall term of school had commenced early in September, and Mary was every day expecting to be summoned to take her place in the new house of her father. It was completed, and she had heard her mother say, the furniture and carpets, which had been purchased in Boston, had arrived, and a day or two would suffice to put everything in order.

Arrangements had been made to continue Mary, as a day scholar, with Madame Robert, and Mary's trunks were packed in anticipation of being sent to the new room, which she had not yet seen. It was a very sultry morning, soon after the opening of school, and all the pupils in the two large rooms at Madame Robert's were busily engaged in writing. Not a sound was heard, except that caused by the many busy pens. Madame Robert, with silent step, glided from one young lady to another, examining her penmanship, and in whispers, commending this one, and suggesting an improvement to another.

A servant tapped on the open door, Madame advanced to the servant, who remained standing in the hall, received from her hands a note, read its superscription, and walking across the room, handed it to Mary Lincoln. With a tremor Mary opened the note, which was from her father, read what she expected, that she must quit boarding school on that day; gave the lines to Madame Robert to read, and feeling only that she was to leave the home of one who had always been kind to her, laid her head on her desk, while large tears coursed down her cheeks.

Madame Robert took her handkerchief, silently raised Mary's head from the desk, wiped her tears, kissed her and left the room. This quiet scene happening in one hidden corner, was not witnessed by many of Mary's companions.

CHAPTER X.

LATE in the afternoon of that warm September day, while teachers and scholars had gone for their daily walk, Mary softly closed the great front-door of Madame Robert's dwelling, and turned her face toward the neighborhood of her father's house. The slanting rays of the evening sun glistened on the glossy motionless leaves of the long lines of silver poplars that shaded both sides of the closely-built street, and glared on the hot staring windows opposite. The air was sultry, and Mary thought betokened a storm. Her soul was sultry also, and she knew the dark clouds were coming up and overshadowing her, and she dreaded the wind and the rain. In vain she wooed the sun; clouds would gather in her prophetic soul, and with lagging step she wended her slow way along. As the familiar tones of a flute, played by one she knew well, came rising and swelling in the evening air, and now floated off and died away, she smiled sadly as she said, "It is a requiem to my happiness. Yes! happiness lies buried for me from henceforth, and I go on to new scenes, a new way of living, new persons, and if I mistake not, to griefs, and perhaps life-long regrets." With this gloom on her young spirit, Mary arrived at her father's house; she rang the bell, a neat pretty-looking American girl opened the door. This was one of two domestics, for whom Mrs. Lincoln had sent to New England—both Americans, whom Mrs. Lincoln's mother had raised from children, and trained up after her own heart.

Mrs. Lincoln's father and mother had both died two years ago, within a few days of each other, and these girls had since that time lived with a sister of Mrs. Lincoln in Rhode Island.

Mrs. Lincoln met Mary in the hall. Hearing the bell ring, and expecting Mary, Mrs. Lincoln had just quitted the parlor where Mr. Lincoln was hanging the last picture. After the first greeting, she said:

"Mary, I may as well tell you now, there is a side door through which you may go out and come in without taking the girls from their work. As we design keeping two domestics only, we must spare them all unnecessary labor." Bessie heard the command of her mistress, and cast a side-long glance at Mary, as she passed to her apartment.

Mr. Lincoln now came out of the parlor, and, with a smile, asked Mary to walk in and see how she liked the rooms and arrangement, as she had not seen the house since the floors were laid.

The parlors were very pretty indeed—very simple—very different from their old home, when her own mother lived, she thought, but such an air of comfort and modest taste reigned here, that Mary expressed warmly to her father her satisfaction, and he seemed pleased. The two rooms opened into each other by large folding doors: immediately in their rear, and connected with them by a glass door, was the sitting-room, cosy and pretty. Brussels carpets of green and oak covered all three floors, and exquisitely fine lace curtains hung from the gilded cornice. The furniture was carved, burnt, or stained walnut, covered with green plush. Between the windows in the front room was a large mirror in a gilt frame, and beneath it a marble slab; gilt candelabra stood on the mantlepiece in the back parlor, and a pair of large, rare vases in silver stands, and two real bronzes, ornamented the richly carved white marble mantlepiece of the front parlor. In one corner of the back parlor stood a new piano. Mary, all eagerness to try the tone of the instrument, opened it, quickly sat down, and drawing off her gloves, ran her fingers over the keys. The tone was delightful, clear, soft, brilliant. Mary said so, as she turned with gratitude to her father to thank him for his thought of her and his attention to her happiness. His eyes forgot themselves, and shed a look of beaming fondness on her, which did not escape Mrs. Lincoln as he walked toward his wife, and said something about his daughter's proficiency in music. Mrs. Lincoln coldly replied that she knew nothing of music, and, therefore, did not appreciate it.

Mary arose, and with a slight chill closed the piano, and followed her father and mother into the sitting-room and library.

"How very pretty this room is!" said Mary.

There was no bay-window here looking off over broad fields and stately trees, but a fresh little piece of sward shut in by a high iron railing bounded the house on this side, and presented a fresh, attractive spot to the city eye. A small gate in this iron railing was the entrance through which Mary was expected to pass, in coming from the precincts beyond. What most pleased her in the sitting-room, was the black walnut mantlepiece, carved wonderfully well in grape vines and leaves and bunches. The wood work throughout the house was black walnut, highly varnished, and yet giving out a strong odor of turpentine. The somber, but elegantly-chiseled walnut bookcase was filled with new and choice volumes, and a pretty little lounge and the deep arm-chairs covered with green, indicated that one might find quiet and enjoyment here.

Now to the dining-room, and then up to the bed-chambers, Mary wended her way, her father just preceding her. In the second story were four bedrooms, one of which over the dining-room and kitchen, and communicating with the kitchen by back stairs, was to be appropriated to a man servant; one of the others was her mother's and his own; the other two were reserved for visitors. With a slight quivering in his voice, which however Mary did not observe, he led her to the attic, where he said she would find a nice room—her own. In the attic were three chambers, one for the two women servants, one a store closet, and the other her own! As Mr. Lincoln closed the door upon Mary, telling her she had better empty her trunks and put her bureau in order, a rush of indignation swept over her. She stood in the center of the room, whose ceiling almost touched the floor on one side, and whose yellow plastered walls had not so much as one coat of whitewash to take off their glaring ugliness. No fire-place or grate was there—no preparations for winter time, which Mary dreaded and disliked. She opened the door which communicated with the servants' room. A close, un-aired smell greeted her nostrils, and in disgust she said :

"I 'll bar this door, and let no one ever dare to open it. What does she mean, to insult me by put-ting me here close beside her servants in this dreary garret, without comforts for winter, with a scorching sun streaming in here all through the long summer days !"

She looked at the simple new three-ply carpet, at the poor little one-foot square mirror, at the cherry bedstead, the cherry bureau, the cherry washstand with a hole in the top, in which was sunk a stone-china bowl and pitcher, and her breast heaved with anger. With a force of which she did not know her-self capable, she bolted the servants' door, walked to the other door of the room, shut it with a crash, locked it, threw herself on the floor, and burst into tears. The memory of the chamber which her own mother had so delighted to adorn for her ; its painted walls, its rich medallion carpet, its splendid mirror, its elegant curtains, its inviting bed, with the snowy ruffled pillows—all its comforts, all its beauty—and the memory of that mother, and her tenderness, her indulgence, her unvarying affection, swept over her, and with a heart full of misery she cried:

"Oh, mother, mother! why did you leave me all alone in this cold, harsh world?"

A tap at the door, she arose; a second tap, she walked to the washstand; she poured out the water into the coarse bowl, no coarser, no uglier than the one at Madame Robert's, in which so many young ladies performed their morning and evening ablutions; and at this moment this remembrance struck Mary suddenly. She dipped her face in the cooling water, wiped it quickly—another tap—and went to the door. She unlocked and opened it. It was Bessie, sent by Mrs. Lincoln to tell Mary that tea was on the table. "Yes," said Mary, and shut and locked the door again.

"After all," thought Mary, as reason came to her, and anger and pride passed off, "it is neat and good enough for me, I suppose; but how comfortless! how villainously ugly! and how shall I ever entertain Gertrude here, accustomed as she is to so much luxury and beauty? To say the least of it, my new chamber," and she looked round again, "is a disappointment, a terrible disappointment to me."

So saying, Mary dipped her face in the bowl, dashed the water many times into her eyes, wiped her flushed cheeks with one of the new towels which lay neatly folded on the towel-rack just at her hand, looked into the small mirror, and thought she had banished all trace of tears. Down stairs she slowly

went, and into the dining-room, where, already seated
at table, were Mr. and Mrs. Lincoln. As Mary took
her place in the vacant chair at her father's right
hand, she did not fail to observe the exquisitely fine
texture of the snow-white damask cloth, the beautiful
shape and pattern of the rich cut-glass, the inviting
home-made bread, and the delicious fragrance of the
yellow butter. The old family silver, resplendent in
the gas light, seemed to greet her as a familiar friend;
and as she dipped her spoon into her cup of tea, it
seemed to nod her a pleasant welcome.

Mrs. Lincoln glanced at Mary, and read aright her
tell-tale face. Mr. Lincoln did not ask his daughter
how she liked her room. Perhaps, if Mary had
known that her father wished to give her a chamber
in a more agreeable part of the house, but that Mrs.
Lincoln had objected for several reasons, she would
have felt a little more reconciled to her new quarters.

After the meal, which passed almost silently, Mrs.
Lincoln went up stairs to put on her bonnet and mantle for an evening walk, and as she took her husband's
arm at the street door, she reminded Mary that it
was time to prepare her lessons for the next day.

Mary gently closed the door behind Mr. and Mrs.
Lincoln, and with a desolate feeling went up to her
room. With a sigh she lighted the gas, took from
her satchel her books, and sat down to study, but not
a breath of air came in at the open window and door,
and the buzz of musquitoes, attracted by the brilliant
light, was so annoying, that Mary threw down her
books, thinking she could study better early the next

morning. As she arose, her open empty bureau and her closed trunks reminded her that she had forgotten to unpack and arrange her clothing. This she now proceeded expeditiously to do, and soon everything was in its proper place.

It was too early to go to bed, and Mary lowered the gas, shut and locked her door, and went to her dormer-window to take a survey of the neighboring house-tops. On tip-toe she raised herself and vainly tried to catch a glimpse of her side of the street; she could see nothing but the row of gas-lights opposite, and the houses with their red brick chimneys, some of which were already going to decay. She smiled almost derisively as she contrasted the limits which bounded her sight to the horizon of Gertrude Clifford. A moment more, and she looked upward at the sky and the stars, and she thought,

"Not much of earth have I here, but as much of heaven as I choose. No matter how weak, or how sinful, or how wretched I am, here, if I desire, I can always see heaven. Who knows," while a hopeful smile passed over her young face, "how soon these dark walls and this lonely window shall make of me an attic philosopher—perhaps a Christian? Who knows but that God will deign to come down to me here, and shed abroad in my poor heart His divine love and His peace!"

CHAPTER XI.

THE next morning, as they rose from the breakfast table, Mrs. Lincoln said, "Mary, your father tells me you were fifteen on your last birthday, and I think it is time you should be initiated into the mysteries of housekeeping. I have set apart for you your own household labors, and I feel I can depend upon you to perform them faithfully."

Mary looked up at her mother with an expression of wonder in her face, and Mrs. Lincoln continued:

"Every morning I wish you to clean your own room, to wash the breakfast things, that is the silver and the glass; dust the parlors, and the sitting-room. On Mondays and Tuesdays, when the servants are more than usually busy, in addition to this you may sweep the dining-room, and on Saturdays you will find it necessary to sweep the parlor and clean the silver."

Mary looked aghast, as she listened to this list of disagreeable duties portioned out for her, and said:

"But, mother, how shall I ever be ready for school; when shall I get my lessons, my French; my German, when shall I study my music; when shall I sew and mend?"

Mr. Lincoln cast a reproving glance at Mary, for her tone was very impatient and quite disrespectful he thought; and Mary's heart swelled as she saw it.

"With patience and perseverance Mary," said Mrs. Lincoln, "you will be able to accomplish much of which you have no idea at present."

"Yes," thought Mary, "and in the accomplishment of such wonders, lose my youth, my hope, perhaps my health, perhaps my life—but who cares; will any one be sad because I am not happy; would not my place be better filled if I were absent?"

"To be a household drudge, of all things in the world! it is a character I despise."

But Mary's own mother had taught her child that obedience to parents was a cardinal virtue, and remembering this, she made an effort to banish these bitter thoughts, to be amiable, to give her new mother as little cause for trouble as possible, and she said meekly:

"I will try to do as you wish me, mother, but really I can not see where I am to find time."

"Allow me to suggest a plan to you, Mary," replied Mrs. Lincoln, "which I am sure you will find practicable, and which, if followed, will make these duties plain to you, and easily performed. Rise early in the morning; after you are dressed, take the bed clothes from off your bed, and turn the mattress so that all may well air; then dust the parlors and sitting-room, which Bessie will see are opened and ready for you; then make your bed and arrange your own room. After breakfast, which meal we shall take precisely at seven, you may wash the 'breakfast things,' and afterward you will have sufficient time to prepare yourself for school.   As you will be at home every afternoon by three o'clock, the intervening hours until tea, are yours, to study your lessons for the next day.   In the evening you will practice your music; on Saturday afternoons you can mend, and sew.   I have no doubt these household employments will seem at first arduous, but I think when you have once learned them you will find them healthful and agreeable."

This pleasing idea, Mary could not comprehend, and she went to school with a heavy heart.

All day she was distraite, pre-occupied.

Madame Robert would have been displeased at the random answers she gave in her recitations, had it not been an occurrence so unusual; as it was she could only, divining the cause of this distraction, regard her beloved pupil with a deeper interest, and a tenderer love, mingled with compassion.

During the half hour of intermission which always commenced at twelve o'clock, Mary, instead of joining her young companions on the back porch, or in the garden behind the house, kept her place at her desk.   When they wondered she did not come, and why she declined their invitation, she said she had a headache; that convenient malady, whose imaginary pains so often serve as a cloak to cover up a whole catalogue of ills of body or mind.   The truth is, she was thinking so intently of her new duties that to-day she could remember nothing else.

Mary Lincoln so highly esteemed intellect, genius, all those noble qualities of mind that make men immortal, and her mother had so often taught her that next to piety and health, the cultivation of her own powers was absolutely necessary, so that she might understand and appreciate those which God had wonderfully bestowed upon a few chosen ones—so that should circumstances throw her among the gifted, she might not be wholly unworthy to mingle her thoughts and words with theirs, at least that she might derive from them instruction, profit, and delight—that a good education above all things had been the ambition of her young life. To see her time so suddenly, so rudely broken in upon, and by occupations so trifling, so distasteful from her present point of view, she considered a great evil. Discouraged by the unpleasant appearance of her future horizon, and by the thought that it would be impossible to do all *well* (and her motto was to endeavor to be persevering and thorough in all she undertook), she felt that to insure peace at home, and perhaps gain the love of her new relative, which was absolutely necessary to her happiness, she must sacrifice part of her studies. This conclusion filled her with melancholy, but young, ardent, brave, energetic as she was, she did not long despond. Roused by the thought of how much can be accomplished by a proper use of every moment of time, she resolved at least to try courageously.

A great weight was lifted from her heart, as she thought, " We are usually such a quiet family, keep such good hours, why can not I retire very early and rise so much earlier in the morning, finding time not only for morning duties, but for the prayer my good mother seemed to forget when she portioned out to me the labors of each hour." "Perhaps," said she a little bitterly, "she thinks I can pray when I do my work; perhaps it is a part of her creed to pray always, to pray without ceasing; and certainly," she continued, "if ever young girl in the beginning of her sixteenth year had need of prayer, daily, constant, I am that one. And I will also," she thought, banishing with an effort gloomy imaginations, "look over my lessons in the fresh morning hours—thus I shall be better able to retain them."

With a lighter step and a more cheerful countenance, she wended her way homeward, and a hopeful face at tea was the result of these reflections.

Unknown to herself, Mary possessed great executive powers. As she commenced the plan laid down for her by her mother, it seemed so easy of accomplishment, that she smiled to herself as she suddenly beheld the great mountain dwindle down to a mole-hill. It is true, there were times as the days grew shorter and winter came on, when these daily duties seemed to drag, and she was sometimes late at school, although her lessons were never neglected.

One Saturday morning, Mrs. Lincoln quietly remarked:

"Mary, the silver was badly cleaned on last Saturday; I hope you will take more pains with it this week. If there is anything disgusting to me, it is dirty silver—and if you look in one of the dining-room closets, you will see any quantity of cobwebs. Do not forget them to-day !"

Mary was mortified, as her mother intended she should be, and wished Mrs. Lincoln had waited and reproved her after her father had gone to his office.

That night, as Mary went up to her father to receive his good-night kiss, he turned coldly away from her, and said :

Mary, you are too old to kiss me now; in future, I beg you will lay aside all such civilities !"

Shocked and pained by these words, Mary went fairly tottering to her room. It seemed, such a weight was on her heart, as if she should never again breathe freely; as if, indeed, her heart was almost all gone. The sweet, soft, rich embrace of her father, to which through every long day she looked forward—the balm to her wounded spirit, the comfort in her griefs, the soother of her petty annoyances, so little to him, so very much to her—to be from henceforth denied her, it was a punishment too great for neglected duties unintentionally slighted. She felt that, next to the death of her mother and her darling Bertha, this was the greatest sorrow of her life. In the dark she threw herself on her knees beside her bed, and her slight figure quivered with pain. Sobs came to her relief, and between them broken snatches of prayer that she might no longer live, that God would in mercy accept her, and take her to himself, for life was no longer valuable. And then arose that inconceivable longing for her own dear mother, for the tender love that made her young days so rich, so sweet, and with outstretched arms she implored, if such could be, the presence of her dead mother.

Oh, daughters! ye who rejoice in the depth and fullness of a mother's love, value that love more than your own life, and while you pity those unfortunate ones who must live on from day to day, from year to year, without the sympathy of their only true friend, thank God heartily for his unspeakable goodness to you. Honor every hair of your mother's head; let not the winds of life blow roughly about her, or the sun scorch her path; plant flowers of beauty and of perfume in her way; ever be watchful and careful of her health, of her happiness, of her comfort, not only that your days may be long in the land which the Lord your God giveth you, but that the light of joy may illume her soul!

Mr. Lincoln felt that he had amply punished Mary for what he supposed her derelictions of duty, and shown to his wife how much he appreciated her endeavors to make his daughter faithfully perform her allotted tasks.

CHAPTER XII.

A WEEK after this occurrence, as Mary sat at the dining-room table, busily cleaning the silver, her mother near her embroidering, Bessie came in and handed Mary a note; she quickly broke the seal, and read aloud:

FRANKLIN HOTEL.

MY DARLING—We have just arrived. Papa wishes to go immediately to the country; but I can not endure the thought of passing another day without seeing you. If agreeable to Mr. and Mrs. Lincoln, I will make you a short visit, and will come in the course of an hour. GERTRUDE.

As Mary finished reading, she looked at Mrs. Lincoln, who said, " Certainly, Mary. We shall be most happy to entertain Gertrude, and you must let Bessie finish your work, and go immediately and return with your friend."

Mary heartily thanked her mother, drew off her working-gloves, and with a light heart bounded up stairs, doffed her morning-dress and apron, donned her street dress, her mantle and bonnet, and started

9

off at a quick pace for the hotel, which was not many
squares from her father's house.

Mr. Clifford and Gertrude had been absent several
months: they had left home, in company with Mr.
and Mrs. Day, for an eastern trip; and Mary's last
letter from Gertrude had mentioned their idea of
returning speedily, but not quite so soon as this. A
few moments and Mary was folded in the embrace of
her friend. Mr. Clifford bade both our young friends
a hasty adieu, saying, his buggy and horses were
waiting at the door of the hotel, and he would take
Gertrude's small carpet-bag and leave it at Mr. Lincoln's, on his way out of town.

It was a lovely October day. Gertrude asked innumerable questions about their mutual friends, Caroline Thomas and Kate Lee, which questions Mary
could not answer very satisfactorily, for, in the new
régime, she was not allowed to go out often or receive
many visitors. Gertrude was about to propose they
should go to see them on their way home, but concluded it would be impolite not to pay her respects
first to Mrs. Lincoln, particularly as they could call
upon their friends this afternoon.

Mr. and Mrs. Lincoln were unusually polite to Gertrude, and welcomed her with great cordiality.

Soon after dinner the two friends set out on their
afternoon tour: they were fortunate in finding Carrie
at the house of Kate, and both, of course, charmed to
see them. They showered upon Gertrude a thousand
questions; but she in her turn had some information

to ask of Kate, which the latter blushed not a little in giving.

Gertrude, at Rye Beach, had met a Mr. Laralde, a gentleman who had spoken with great admiration of Kate; and as Kate had never mentioned him, Gertrude thought it a singular circumstance. Kate acknowledged a slight acquaintance with him, and blushed again, when Gertrude remarked that he had told her of his intention of establishing himself permanently in their city; and then Gertrude, with so much warmth, depicted this gentleman's appearance, that Kate's face fairly glowed with interest and pleasure.

"What a splendid brow," said she; "so white, so broad—and such silky brown hair! What a depth of power, of intellect in those clear, blue eyes! and he wears no beard either, which absence gives to view his beautiful rounded chin! Oh! comme il est beau! comme il est spirituel! comme il est élégant! n'est ce pas ma chère Katie!" turning suddenly to Kate, who replied:

"On le croirait bien à vous entendre parler de cette façon."

Mary did not take much interest in the conversation, except to observe the tell-tale blushes of Katie's face.

After they bade adieu to Carrie and Katie, they continued their promenade in another direction.

Oh! those delightful hours of blooming maidens, when, fresh and young, untrammeled by care, untainted by worldliness, they stroll along through the busy street, stopping to look in at tempting windows, to admire laces and the latest style of dress goods, or new paintings and engravings, or new bonnets, or whatever else is arranged to attract the taste, or create new desires, or draw forth from the pocket the well-filled purse. To-day Gertrude had no wants; every preparation, in the way of dress—every purchase, for the winter season, had been made in New York—and, as to Mary, her attenuated porte-monnaie boasted no sum sufficient to gratify her wants, if, unluckily, she had had any.

On they walked, in sweet converse, stopping now to admire the almost palatial residences in this part of the city—the rich green grass-plats, the blooming fall flowers and green shrubs in the small gardens which decorated many of these dwellings. How fresh and delicious was the air here! how soft the sunshine! the glimpses of the sky, how much broader as they advanced to where the houses stood farther apart! Mary caught Gertrude's joyous spirit, and forgot she had ever known a pang.

They returned in time for tea, cheeks glowing with healthy exercise — eyes sparkling with cheerfulness.

But if Mrs. Lincoln imagined, for a moment, that Mary had confided her troubles to Gertrude, she was mistaken, for Mary had not mentioned her name, except in terms of the highest commendation.

As Mrs. Lincoln was about to retire for the night, she said:

"I am sure, you are fatigued, Miss Clifford, after your long journey, and, whenever you wish to go to bed, Mary will attend you to your chamber." And then, turning to Mary: "Miss Clifford will occupy the room next to mine."

"Oh, no!" said Gertrude quickly; "I do not intend to make you any trouble at all. I very much prefer sharing Mary's room to-night. I beg you will not give me a room all to myself."

"Very well, then," said Mrs. Lincoln, with the slightest perceptible shade in her voice, "if you prefer sharing Mary's accommodations, you can do so, as I am sure she will be glad of your company."

"Certainly, dear Gertrude," said Mary, "and as I see your eyelids droop a little, we will go now, if you please."

Gertrude rose and kissed Mrs. Lincoln good-night, and shook hands gracefully with Mr. Lincoln. Mary kissed Mrs. Lincoln, too, said "good-night, father," and all left the sitting-room.

As Mary turned on the gas in her room, while Gertrude entered; happily she did not see the start of surprise which escaped her friend, but which was immediately concealed.

"Dear Gertrude," said Mary, with slight irony in her tone, "let me introduce you to my new apartment. As it is so large, I have thought best to divide it into several compartments. There, on the north end, is my drawing-room; which fact you might not be able to comprehend, were it not for the marble statuettes you see on their brackets of rosewood, which brackets, with this small table whereon is my writing-desk, and this little chair, are quite recent acquisitions. The south end of the chamber is my bedroom—witness my bed and washstand, with the admirable mirror which hangs above the latter-named object; and here, within the recess which this dormer-window forms, is my library. This is my sanctum of sanctums, where I sit gazing at the anti-quated red chimneys opposite, or, inspired by their poetical presence, I write an essay for Madame Robert's composition day, or study my lessons, or dream fantastic dreams over my needle."

And as Gertrude opened wide her eyes, Mary laughed a merry peal, which sounded startlingly in that quiet hour and place. Then, gently drawing Gertrude into the small recess she had named her library, she said:

"Dear Gertrude, there is here room enough for you as well as myself, and, while I have consecrated to you many a sweet thought between and underneath these yellow walls, deign to enter, that I may tell you, from henceforth I hope to receive you here often—very often. I shall dedicate this spot to love and Gertrude."

"I am greatly honored," replied Mary's friend, as with a sweet smile she bent low her peerless head, "but let me request, my darling, you will dedicate it not only to affection for me," and she embraced Mary warmly, "but also to poetry, to religion, to philoso-phy. What a charming little boudoir it will then be, and instructive as well as delightful. Here I see my loved young friend, filled with the refined tastes, wrapped in the sweet thoughts God has given her,

tracing on these walls the beautiful sentiments of an
admired author, or, still better, her own."

"Thank you, Gertrude, for your suggestion," said
Mary, "believe me, I shall soon put it in execution;
and who knows but these walls, formerly so revolting,
shall soon sparkle and glow with the rich sayings of
mighty masters, old and young.   Here will I also keep
my diary, and no one but Gertrude shall see it—for
other steps never enter here.   Expect to have served
up to you, at your next visit, Miss Clifford, an intellectual olla podrida."

"Thank you again and again, dear Gertrude; in a
moment you have changed the aspect of my dreary
room, and from henceforth, in my eyes, it will possess
the greatest interest."

CHAPTER XIII.

THE ensuing winter passed monotonously away for Mary, but in the house there was cheerfulness, even gayety. Mrs. Lincoln entertained a great deal, generally acquaintances from the East, on their way to the West or South. Upon reception of the cards of such persons, she hastened with alacrity to pay her respects to them, and with cordial hospitality invited them to dine, or sup, or pass under her roof such time as they might find convenient or agreeable. Mary pursued her studies with ardor, in one corner of her mother's chamber, under the gas light, or near the blazing coal fire; another time, perhaps in the dining-room, after the tea things had been removed, with her book in hand, she conned her delightful tasks, or with measured steps she paced the floor, repeating aloud sentences which particularly attracted her attention. Sometimes the low hum of voices in the parlor below distracted, for a time, her studious thoughts; sometimes music, vocal or instrumental, caused her to throw down her book with a sudden start; sometimes she was called to take her part in the entertainment, which she did so far better than any one else there, calling forth such encomiums upon her exquisite touch, upon her grace of execution, upon her taste, as soon convinced Mrs. Lincoln, novice as she was in the art, that her husband's daughter was an accomplished musician. Sometimes, when there were not many guests at table, Mary joined them, and listened delightedly to the narratives of traveled men and women, to

"The perils braved, the strange new objects seen
That prompt the inquiry keen of envying sages;"

Or she drank in inspiration from the intellectual fountains thus opened to her; and as she saw the sparkling eye of her father, and caught on his face the emotion which revealed so plainly his delight, his admiration of a passage more than usually eloquent, she desired more than ever a cultivated mind, and she determined, God willing, that one day he should pay *her* the same tribute of admiration. She still longed for his love—oh how intensely! She besought God every hour of her life that He would grant her this great boon, that He would also grant her the love of her mother. Her heart panted for love, and yet it seemed denied her. The affection of Gertrude was a solace to her; cheered many a dark hour, but it was particularly the love of those in her father's house for which she prayed and pined. All were so cold here, even the servants. Mrs. Lincoln never forgot herself so far as to give her husband the slightest caress; Mr. Lincoln so far laid aside his dignity as to bestow occasionally a kiss upon his wife, but poor Mary never

received a word, a sign, not even the " sweet assurance
of a look " from any one under her father's roof.

But this dearth, so long her portion, was made up
to her in her spiritual life. God seemed always near
her. He was indeed her refuge, a very present help
in time of need. She rejoiced in the thought that
His love was not unattainable, and that divine love
was so fully, so entirely granted her, that often, very
often, her soul was lifted up to Him in holy rapture.
Gratefully she thanked Him for His gifts, for this
beautiful world, for the song of birds, the fragrance
and loveliness of flowers, for the mountain and the
valley, the river and the rivulet, the sun, the moon,
and the stars, the gentle winds of heaven: for health
and home, and friends, her darling Gertrude, and her
dear Mrs. Day. She thanked Him for the tastes He
had implanted in the souls of men, for genius, for intellect, for wisdom, and more than all for his greatest
gift—the gift of the Divine Savior. And in the silent watches of the night, she talked with Him, as
with her best friend; she told him her sorrows, she
laid open to Him her griefs, she prayed to bear all
patiently and meekly; she prayed to be a true Christian, that she might be guided rightly; that hers
might not be a " religion of taste," flattering itself
a Christian when God was far from its thoughts. She
desired to honor Him, to glorify Him always in every
deed, and that love to Him might be the main-spring
of all her actions. And every day she was growing
in grace, unfolding in spiritual loveliness, even her
slightest deeds were proof of the efficacy of her pray-

ers. Who in sorrow, in woe, in despair, has ever offered up a fervent petition to Him who sees and watches over all, and not felt when rising from his knees, a load of misery removed? His ear is, indeed, ever open. *His* arm is ever extended to save; with mercy and love in His aspect, He beckons all to come. Let us then with humility approach and receive a blessing! a blessing far beyond price!

It was astonishing that Mrs. Lincoln felt no more tenderness for this gentle being; it is certain, however, that although chary of her words of encouragement and praise, still she admired Mary extremely, and felt that she was wonderfully superior to most girls of her age. She congratulated herself not a little for the excellent qualities, the high principles Mary was every day developing under her direction, for her application to study, her industry, especially for the economy which poor Mary was forced so rigidly to observe.

The writing on the wall had not progressed rapidly of late. The very severe weather this winter had prevented Mary's fully carrying out Gertrude's idea, still there were a few passages which she had hurriedly traced, which gave her much pleasure, and which she always stopped to read before quitting her room. She particularly admired the writings of Longfellow, and some of his beautiful thoughts graced her little sanctum. Among them:

" This life of ours is a wild Æolian harp of many a joyous strain,
   But under them all there runs a loud, perpetual wail, as of souls in
   pain."

And :

" All through life there are way-side inns, where man may refresh his
    soul with love :
Even the lowest may quench his thirst at rivulets, fed by springs
    from above.

And :

> " Darker, darker and more wan
>   In my breast the shadows fall :
> Upward steals the life of man
>   As the sunshine from the wall:
> From the wall into the sky,
>   From the roof along the spire,
> All the souls of those that die
>   Are but sunbeams lifted higher."

And :

> " O, what a glory does this world put on
>   For him who, with a fervent heart goes forth
> Under the bright and glorious sky, and looks
>   On duties well-performed and days well spent."

Gertrude was honored too, for from one of her letters
Mary had culled this sentiment :

"That freedom from earthly sorrows which beguiles the soul of
its conscious destination, its soaring prerogatives, is nothing but a
curse."

And from Miss Bremer :

"The day of heavy sighs is not passed; and it will not have
passed until the last day of the world."

From Walter Scott :

" Adversity is like the period of the former and the latter rain—

cold, comfortless, unfriendly to man and to animal; yet from that season have their birth, the flower and the fruit, the date, the rose, and the pomegranate."

From different authors, Mary selected many more quotations — always found something on her wall suited to every phase of feeling—and thus was her immovable scrap-book not only a pleasure in happy hours, but also a solace in dark ones.

Her school-days were now fast drawing to a close. Mrs. Lincoln thought that, as she had left school early (at sixteen), and as Mary was rapidly approaching seventeen, she might now quit Madame Robert, particularly as Mr. Lincoln had a friend, a professor of the dead languages, who was under obligations to him in the way of money, and who desired to return, at least, a part, by giving Mary Latin lessons.

It was therefore settled that, in February, Mary should take her leave of school days; and before she commenced with Mr. Droune, her father proposed to take her with him to New Orleans, as he intended going there on business, and would stay there long enough to allow Mary to see something of the city. Some friends of his were also going, and Mary was in a fever of delight. Mrs. Lincoln demurred a little; she had declined Mr. Lincoln's invitation herself, as she did not like steamboats, but, after a short time, as the day for their departure advanced, she aided Mary kindly in her preparations, and even insisted upon adding to her wardrobe by lending her some fine laces and embroideries. Mary was truly glad and grateful.

An hour or two before Mr. Lincoln and Mary went down to the boat which was to convey them, Mrs. Lincoln, handing a letter to Mr. Lincoln, said:

"Mr. Lincoln, I do not know that I have ever spoken to you of a distant cousin of mine, Mr. Dana, who lives in New Orleans: do me the favor, if you please, to take this letter of introduction to him. You will find him a very agreeable gentleman."

Mary enjoyed every moment of her trip. The first time she had ever been so far from home, sights and scenes so new filled her with constant excitement. Mr. Lincoln observed the radiant expression of her countenance, and congratulated himself upon the pleasure he was giving her. His manner to his daughter was very kind, but still that great wall of reserve, built up between them, Mary feared would never be thrown down. When they left home, the river was filled with floating pieces of ice; in a day or two, all traces of a cold region had disappeared; a day or two again, nature was budding and green, in all the freshness and beauty of an early spring; and still later, one would have thought that cold airs and nipping frosts never came to this salubrious region.

One day, before they reached New Orleans, when they had stopped to wood, their whole party visited a plantation on the coast. The gentlemanly master (who was on the portico of his house, as they approached, and whom one of their number accosted, desiring permission to view his place) invited them to enter, and led the way to the gate which separated

the orange-grove from the other parts of his planta-
tation. As all stepped within the barrier, what exclamations of delight burst from the ladies especially, at sight of the exquisite hedge of roses which
completely shut in this little Eden. Mary could
scarcely tell which to admire most, the roses blooming
in every hue and shape, or the magnificent orange-
trees, laden with flowers, and green and ripe fruit. On
the ground, at their feet, lay immense golden oranges,
nestling in the rich, soft grass ; and as the proprietor
of this fairy place desired all to help themselves to as
many flowers and as much fruit as they wished, they
were not dilatory in accepting his invitation. Mary
felt that she was treading on fairy ground, or dreaming, perhaps, and might wake too suddenly and rudely
from the spell.

But now they heard the first warning tap of the
boat's bell, and turned to express their gratitude to
their stranger host. As he stood at the gate, and
they all passed out with a few words of compliment,
Mary, in her turn, said:

"You have indeed, sir, given me more pleasure,
to-day, than I ever before experienced in so short a
time—a pleasure, too, so novel, and which I shall never
forget."

The gentleman bowed and cordially shook Mary's
proffered hand, while Mr. Lincoln wondered to hear
his daughter say so much. As the party neared the
house, Mary discovered, at a little distance, an old
negro woman picking moss. She slipped quietly
from her friends, and put a half dollar into old aunty's

hands, who was so taken by surprise, that she forgot to say, "Thank'ee, young missus!" until Mary was far beyond hearing.

The next evening, as the boat approached New Orleans, and they were all on deck, Mary caught her first glimpse of a sloop, sailing quietly and majestically toward them, and, in the stillness of that hour, when there was no sound except the puffing of the steam of the boat—and as the sun sank behind the low shores, and its long light streamed in rich purple and gold across the water—and as gay ladies, richly dressed, promenaded the low banks which lined both sides of the river, and as white-headed old negroes leaned meditatively over fences, to watch them as they passed, how Mary started from her pleasant reveries to hear an old lady say, as vessels came gliding toward them : "Do look! do look! how they swim! *exactly* like a duck!"

Soon darkness succeeded to twilight, and as they approached the Crescent city, thousands of gaslights started up and glimmered in every direction. A week of intense enjoyment followed; and as at the door of the St. Charles Hotel Mr. Lincoln and Mary were just stepping into the carriage which was to convey them to the boat, their visit to New Orleans ended, a gentleman came rushing toward them in great haste.

"Is this Mr. Lincoln—is this Miss Lincoln," said he, all out of breath; "and you are not going to leave so soon, I hope! Permit me!—I am Mr. Dana, the person to whom Mr. Lincoln brought a letter."

"If you have time," said Mr. Lincoln, Mary

thought, with a slight touch of sarcasm in his tone, "Mr. Dana, will you not accompany us? We have yet an hour before the boat leaves,"—looking at his watch.

"Thank you," replied Mr. Dana, as he helped Mary into the carriage, and entered it immediately afterward, followed by Mr. Lincoln, "let me hasten to explain my seeming neglect of Mrs. Lincoln's letter. I have been absent, and returned this morning only, from Texas. Upon going to my office, I found a large package of unopened letters, which my agent had neglected, and, unluckily, the very last one which I took up, was this letter of my cousin. I regret exceedingly my misfortune in seeing so little of you! and, perhaps, I might have been useful to Miss Lincoln;" and he turned to Mary and addressed her:

"Have you been to the opera? have you seen Macready? did you go to Carrollton? did you take a ride on the Shell road? have you been to the Lake? have you looked into Fanny Fry's window? have you been to market? have you heard Dr. Knapp? To all of which questions Mary bent her head with an amused smile.

"I declare it is too bad!" he continued, after some inquiries about Mrs. Lincoln, "how much I have lost by being absent;" and after they reached the boat, while Mr. Lincoln was attending to the baggage, and Mary and Mr. Dana were seated in the ladies' cabin, Mr. Dana suddenly rose and said laughingly to his companion, "can not I do something yet to prevent

10

your going? Can't I disarrange the machinery? Can't I set the boat on fire?"

"Oh! that would be dreadful," said Mary, smiling.

"Can not Mr. Lincoln prolong his stay a few days?" added Mr. Dana, again seating himself beside Mary.

"No," quietly replied Mary, "I heard father say he had an imperative engagement at home, which would not allow him to be absent any longer."

Our friends had a delightful return trip, and found the weather quite mild and pleasant, when they arrived. Mary and her father walked from the river, leaving the baggage to follow.

When they rang the door-bell, Mary could not repress a sigh of regret that she had so soon returned. She dreaded again meeting her mother. She had been so happy while away, had never once thought of little painful domestic incidents that constantly filled her with sadness under her father's roof, that as the peal of that bell sounded on her ear, old memories seemed to revive with it, and the same old feeling that her presence was an indifference to them all, took possession once again of every faculty.

As the front door opened, they caught a glimpse of Mrs. Lincoln in the dining-room, and she saw them enter; she did not advance with glad step to welcome our travelers, but quietly received the embrace of her husband, who walked with light and rapid step to meet her, and without rising from her seat coldly returned that of his daughter.

Mary went up to her desolate room, and at sight of

its dust and its forlornness, threw herself in her little rocking-chair, and indulged in a hearty cry. No kind hand had smoothed her pillows, had with careful neatness made anew her neglected bed, had wiped the dust from chairs and table, and Mary felt bitterly this great inattention to her comfort; she felt like an unwelcome trespasser, and she indulged for hours in this idea. But better thoughts at last came to her; she imagined it ungrateful to her father to return all his kindness and the happiness of the last month in this manner, and so cheered up, endeavoring to make the best of her vexations. Gertrude came to make a visit of a week, and at the end of that time, Mary was quite bright again; she forgot the chilling manner in which her mother had received her, and gave her a merry description of Mr. Dana's call, and told her of the visit to the plantation, and many other incidents to which Mrs. Lincoln listened with evident pleasure.

Soon after her return, Mary commenced Latin with Mr. Droune, and also with the same gentlemen a course of history. These hours were delightful to her, and very instructive. Her awe and veneration of her teacher did not prevent her asking him many questions on all subjects interesting to her, and he, delighted with her capabilities and her anxiety for improvement, gave her much valuable information. Her father also yielded to her desire to again study vocal music, which she had neglected during the last year, and she now began under a competent instructor, with all her old enthusiasm, this charming practice. Thus a few months passed, and Mary absorbed in these pleasures and pursuits, with her old duties, and some new ones added, really quite forgot to be unhappy. . She had given up all hope of the love of her mother, still she did not in the least relax her kindness, or her attention to her wants, and her little comforts; she even seemed to anticipate her desires; she had an intuitive feeling now that her father was a true friend, and felt more for her than he dared express, and thus she went on her way rejoicing—conscience approving all her endeavors.

CHAPTER XIV.

ONE bright morning in the following June, Mary rose early, and went about her usual duties with more than ordinary alacrity. A delicious sense of the luxury of existence permeated her being. The active step, the brilliant eye, the sweet carol that every now and then in snatches gushed from her lips, as she stopped to perform, with unusual care, her pleasant work, revealed a heart at peace with God, with the world and with itself; and as she stood a few moments at the open window, and drank in the beauties of the morning hour, the delicious air, the balmy sunshine which had succeeded the storm of the night before, her young face lighted up with the glow of enjoyment.

I once heard a foreign gentlemen, as full of imagination as he was of wit, of cultivation, of judgment, speaking of how little we can depend upon the promises of certain individuals, remark—"There are days for us all, when it is easy to say 'oui' to everything one demands of us ; days when our sun shines with deeper glory, when the flowers of life send forth a richer fragrance, when filled with tender sentiments, with charmed ideas, forgetful of self, we move on in a halo of purity, an atmosphere of love—communing with the honored dead, or fused, melted as it were, into the hearts of the living—yes! these are our ' oui' days, days whose lasting memory goes on with us to the end of time, whose lasting impression forever engraved upon our hearts, seen through the long vista of departed years, is ever new, and ever fresh, and ever young."

For Mary, this was one of the days when the wayside inns of life were all open, and she entered, refreshing her soul with love, love divine, love unspeakable.

At eight o'clock, she had dressed for the day, in a sweet, simple robe of delicate rose-color, which contrasted well with her black hair and eyes. Her graceful, well-proportioned figure, the sweet expression of her gentle countenance, her quiet, easy, dignified manners, now often drew comments of admiration from all her friends, and from many a stranger, gazing at her for the first time.

A little later in the day, she sat in Mrs. Lincoln's room, reading aloud, as was her usual custom one or two hours every morning, and while her mother knit or embroidered, Mary would sometimes stop and ask a question, or would listen for moments (rapt) to her clear, concise explanations of the subject under notice. Sometimes they would both discuss historical events ; for history, connected with biography and poetry, was the course of reading marked out for Mary, and Mary did not fail to draw from her mother's valuable store of wisdom, gems of knowledge and pure delight.

All absorbed this morning, as both were in the history of Raphael Sanzio d'Urbino, which Mary for the first time was reading, neither of them saw Bessie (who had entered the room silently), until she said to Mrs. Lincoln (presenting a small silver waiter, on which were two cards), "two gentlemen down stairs, ma'am, who asked for yourself and Miss Mary."

"Say we will be there in a moment," replied Mrs. Lincoln, as Bessie went out of the chamber.

"My cousin Caldwell, and Mr. Dana, of New Orleans, Mary," as she read the cards again. And as with a pleased smile she took up the brush to smooth again her glossy hair, she said, while looking in the glass, "Come down soon, Mary," and tripped away with a light step.

What an involuntary trembling seized our young friend. She had scarcely thought of Mr. Dana since last winter; why should her heart so stir within her now, at the sound of his name. Perhaps, Mary Lincoln, because he was associated with pleasant reminiscences! perhaps—do you believe in presentiments?

She rose, laid down her book, walked across the floor, came back again and sat down; she thought she would not go down stairs, then concluded it would be rude to stay any longer up-stairs, then suddenly left the room and went slowly to the parlor, where her mother and the gentlemen were sitting.

Mr. Caldwell was a cousin of Mrs. Lincoln, from Massachusetts, who had lately come here to reside, and had bought a country seat five or six miles from town, where his family had very recently become established.

As Mary entered, her mother introduced Mr. Dana to her, and she advanced with dignity, but with a smile, saying that if she remembered rightly, she had met Mr. Dana before. Mr. Caldwell seated himself beside her, and engaged her in conversation, while Mrs. Lincoln and Mr. Dana asked and answered questions with amazing rapidity.

Mary did not dare look at Mr. Dana; her heart kept up a quick throbbing, while, in a pause in the conversation, he turned suddenly and said:

"Then, Miss Lincoln, you have not forgotten the day I met you so brusquely in New Orleans?"

"No," said Mary, while a slight tinge passed over her cheek, and her voice trembled so that for a few moments she ceased to talk to Mr. Caldwell.

"Cousin Anna, I hope, excused my apparent neglect of her letter, when she became aware that I was absent when the letter arrived.

Mrs. Lincoln replied, that she was disappointed when she heard her husband and daughter had seen so little of Mr. Dana during their visit, but was glad they were so fortunate as to have met him even for a moment before quitting New Orleans.

"I can assure you I was out of humor with myself and everything around me for a month afterward, because of my unlucky fate," said Mr. Dana.

"I hope your temper was not seriously impaired?" said Mary, taking courage to speak, while a bright smile flitted over her young face.

"Those with whom I have been in constant contact will be able to answer this question more truly than I can, Miss Lincoln," said Mr. Dana. "My friends do sometimes accuse me of being less amiable than formerly."

"It is unfortunate," said Mary, in a tone of playfulness, "to have one's temper marred for so slight a cause."

"I have no doubt my present visit," said Mr. Dana, "will quite restore me to myself again. I expect much from my cousin's gentle influences," bowing to Mrs. Lincoln, "they used to be so salutary."

"And, perhaps," thought Mrs. Lincoln, "he trusts slightly to other gentle influences than mine," as she bowed low to Mr. Dana's compliment.

The gentlemen now rose to go. Mr. Dana declined Mrs. Lincoln's invitation to dinner, as he was already engaged elsewhere, but with great apparent pleasure accepted one to tea. He spoke of desiring to call upon Mrs. Caldwell, but Mrs. Lincoln wished him to put off that visit until the following morning, and she would be happy to accompany him.

A short time before, Mr. Lincoln had presented her with an elegant coach and horses, and, with a little pride, Mrs. Lincoln thought how pleasant it would be to show off her handsome attelage to Mr. Dana.

With more care than usual, Mary dressed herself for the evening, and early in the afternoon her mother and herself descended to the sitting-room. Mrs. Lincoln took from her pretty little basket her work and embroidering materials, while Mary, from her

11

own basket—a prized gift from Gertrude—drew forth
a long strip of linen cambric to be transformed into
wonderfully beautiful little ruffles. Mr. Dana soon
arrived, fresh and beaming. He did not talk much
to Mary, but placed himself on the low sofa, close by
Mrs. Lincoln's side, and seemed very happy in re-
calling old days and pleasant memories.

Mary was all engrossed by her work, at least she
thought so, although her ear was involuntarily attracted by the rich voice of Mr. Dana. Could she
have seen the glances his blue eyes darted stealthily
at her, as she sat there in her maidenly freshness, the
sweet look of retiring modesty and dignity on her
brow, as her slender fingers drew the dainty needle
and thread industriously through the delicate fabric,
the throbbing at her heart would have quickened
even more than now. Oh! Mary, Mary, why does
this stranger, this total stranger to you, so stir your
heart with gentle thoughts!

Lately Mrs. Lincoln has opened her house to your
young friends, and many men of talent, of intellect,
delight to enter here, not only charmed with the
friendly manners, and the agreeable conversation of
the mistress, but won by the quiet simplicity of the
young daughter. Some have even gone so far as to
lay at your feet, the greatest compliment in their
power, a compliment to which you have tremblingly
and unwillingly listened, and rejected gently, but
sadly, perhaps, sometimes pityingly.

Why are you, then, so soon taken captive by one
whom you have scarcely seen at all? Why, as the

tones of his voice fall on your ear, are you filled with a pleasurable glow, a quiet happiness, a thrill, so new, so incomprehensible?

Mrs. Lincoln quitted the room at Bessie's unusual summons, and Mr. Dana rose, drew an ottoman close to Mary's feet, and sat down beside her. Her heart fluttered, but she controlled every appearance of agitation.

He asked her what she was making so fine, so delicate; he examined the stitches, which, he said, he could not see at all; he declared her a wonderfully expert work-woman, and when she smiled incredulously, he laughed and said he was a good practical judge, that if she still doubted, would she not permit him to convince her by allowing him to sew a little on this same needlework! She gracefully yielded him the morsel of linen cambric, and put the very fine needle and thread in his great man's fingers, and as he held out his hand for her delicate little gold thimble, another gift of Gertrude, she trembled all over, as she endeavored, unsuccessfully, to put it on, while she laughingly declared it would not fit even his smallest finger. Then he concluded he could sew quite as well without a thimble, and acknowledged he was not accustomed to using the article, while he busily turned anew the hem, and tried to draw the needle through the cobweb-like stuff. But the needle adroitly slipped through his fingers at every attempt to hold it, or the thread knotted and snarled, and Mary cried out—

"Oh, Mr. Dana, my poor work will be ruined; only

see what a hem you have made and how you have
drawn up my last stitches. Now, confess yourself a
novice in this art, and also that you are an incapable
judge."

"I see I must give up my pretensions to any knowledge of this womanly mystery, but I still declare I
am capable of giving an opinion, and that you sew
beautifully, Miss Mary—does she not cousin Anna?"
said Mr. Dana, as Mrs. Lincoln entered, and he rose
from his low seat and walked across the floor.

"Mary does everything well," said Mrs. Lincoln.

It was the first word of commendation Mary
had ever received from this source. Startled, surprised, gladdened by these kind words, Mary could
have embraced her mother. As it was, she looked
up, while a tear-drop gathered in her eye, and forgetting time, and place, and all except those delightful
words, said, cordially—

"Thank you, dear mamma."

At tea, Mr. Lincoln was unusually reserved, while
Mrs. Lincoln's spirits were never more buoyant;
her thoughts never more glittering. Mary was silent,
as she always was at table, and listened quietly to the
conversation.

In a pause she inadvertently looked up at Mr.
Dana, who sat opposite. His eyes were resting on
her, with such an expression of admiration, of tenderness, as made her eyelids droop in quick confusion.
Mr. and Mrs. Lincoln both happened, at the same
moment, to look up also, and both noted that glance.

Mrs. Lincoln with proud satisfaction, while Mr. Lincoln experienced quite a different emotion.

After tea, they went into the back parlor. Mr. Dana and Mr. Lincoln happily did not smoke, and Mrs. Lincoln and Mary again resumed their work. Mr. Lincoln protested against their doing such fine sewing by gaslight, as he declared it very injurious to the eyes, and Mary folded up hers and laid it in the work basket at her side.

Mr. Lincoln and Mr. Dana were soon talking politics quite warmly, luckily agreeing, and Mrs. Lincoln joined them, while Mary listened, interested, but every now and then feeling a slight quiver of disapprobation, as her mother, with brilliant eyes, with rosy cheeks, and an excited manner, uttered a more than usually fervent expression or sentence. Mary did not like to hear women talk politics. "We are not allowed to vote," she thought, "and I am sure no true, high minded woman, however much of a 'woman's rights' person she may be, would desire to interfere in what is exclusively the province of man. It is all well enough to know what is going on in our country, to understand every political question, indeed I am sure it is important, and if we do not possess patriotism, we should cultivate it; but I always blush for a woman who talks upon these subjects in a loud, masculine voice and manner, and I feel like repeating to her what Napoleon said to Madame De Staël, 'Women should *knit*, Madame, and not talk politics!'" Mr. Dana, in a nervous way, changed his seat from one chair to another, and at last, in a lull of conversation, rising and approaching the piano, said, in a quiet voice:

"This open instrument, and this scattered music, betoken, I am sure, that some one in the house, devotes at least a part of her time to one of the joys of life—as I am a prophet as well as a practical judge of needlework, I divine that it is Miss Lincoln who plays; am I not correct, cousin Anna?" (Mrs. Lincoln smilingly nodded.) "As I am one of those 'moved by the concord of sweet sounds,' I beseech Miss Mary to perform for my pleasure, and my profit," and he advanced to where Mary sat, who quietly rose, and stood by the piano while Mr. Dana placed the stool for her.

"Instrumental or vocal music, shall it be?" said Mary, without looking up, while she arranged the scattered leaves upon the piano.

"Begin with a piece of your own selection, if you please," said Mr. Dana. "Anything you like; your favorite morceau will be something worth hearing, I am sure."

"They are all favorites of mine, Mr. Dana," said Mary.

"Are you, then, so fond of music?" he asked.

"Oh, very fond of it," responded Mary, as her fingers, with silver touch, drew forth from the instrument a few solemn, minor sounds, and then changing the key, darted off into such a brilliant, easy, graceful, gay, dashing air, then trilling most wonderfully, with her right hand, while, with her left, she carried a majestic melody, that the man beside her scarcely knew whether he was in heaven, or suspended in the air. Mr. Lincoln always listened to his daughter's astonishing music with increasing pleasure, and could not shut his eyes to its power on Mr. Dana. Shall we say that a pang shot through his heart as he gazed on that face lighted up with inspiration, with delight, and as he caught the sigh which escaped his guest when the rippling, dying notes concluded the magic melody.

When Mary had finished, Mr. Dana said nothing; he walked up and down the rooms and came to the piano where she still sat, turning over the leaves of an old music book, and asked her to sing.

And while she sang, ballad after ballad, in her clear young voice, with all her heart, with all her soul, with deep, with tender pathos, he bent over her, absorbed, lost to all, except that celestial voice, except to the thought that he was close beside one, he knew so sweet, so good, so lovely; and she, too, felt—oh, Mary Lincoln! she, too, realized nothing but that he stood near her, overshadowing her, he who seemed a life time friend, whose tone made every pulse beat with gladness, whose look sent a thrill to the very depths of her heart, whose presence filled her with joy unspeakable. She sang, tireless, until a late hour, and Mr. Dana said he must tear himself away. As he bade them good night, Mrs. Lincoln reminded him of the visit they were to pay on the morrow to Mrs. Caldwell, and told him she would call for him in her carriage at his hotel, or wherever he desired. He thanked her politely and said he would not give her so much trouble, but would come to her house at at any time she preferred. She fixed upon half past nine the next day, and he took his leave.

CHAPTER XV.

At the breakfast table, the following day, Mrs. Lincoln remembered that she had made a previous engagement for this morning, and she asked Mr. Lincoln if he would permit Mary to accompany Mr. Dana in her place, as she felt mortified at the idea of disappointing him. Mary gave a slight start at this proposition of her mother, and the deepest crimson suffused her cheeks. Mr. Lincoln assented politely, but not with cheerful alacrity.

Half past nine o'clock came and with it the carriage, and a moment after, Mr. Dana. Mrs. Lincoln and Mary were both in the parlor, both in visiting toilette. While Mary was dressing, she had once or twice asked herself, with a blush, if it was quite delicate that Mrs. Lincoln should transfer this engagement to her; but Mrs. Lincoln's previous engagement, and Mr. Dana's short stay, seemed to her at last, sufficient excuses.

After Mr. Dana had sat for a few moments, Mrs. Lincoln began to explain to him the reasons for failing in the appointment she had made with him the day before, and to tell him of the present plan. Mary had risen and was nervously sorting her loose music, so that she did not see the changing expressions on the countenance of the gentleman. Mrs. Lincoln did not feel highly complimented, as the disappointment his face first evidenced turned to a look of radiant pleasure.

As Mr. Dana handed Mary to the coach and took his seat opposite her, Mrs. Lincoln bade them good morning and an agreeable ride, and then tripped off down street, chuckling to herself at the thought of her excellent management.

The morning was lovely—was delightful—and as they rode along and left the city and its suburbs, and began to climb the high hills from whence they had charming glimpses of the valleys below, and the far off city which gradually faded entirely from the sight, and green hills and lovely cottages and thick forests succeeded to the view, a quiet sense of delicious happiness filled every pulse of Mary's being. Mr. Dana had so often expressed his admiration of the different pictures they had passed, which admiration many had as often echoed, that now, for a little time, both were silent, apparently drinking in the luxury of the morning.

Suddenly, Mr. Dana said:

"Then, Miss Mary, you have not forgotten the day I met you so abruptly in New Orleans."

"Yes—no!" answered Mary with some trepidation. "Perhaps I might have forgotten it (my memory is so capricious), had it not been for cousin Saunders." Cousin Saunders was a portly old gentleman, very deaf, a relative of Mrs. Lincoln from Mississippi, who had spent a month last spring at Mr. Lincoln's.

"Yes," said Mr. Dana.

And Mary continued—

"Every day, after. dinner, he used to come and whisper in my ears, so loud that all but himself could hear, such pleasant things about Mr. Dana that I was in no danger of forgetting him."

"I hope he did not annoy you!" said Mr. Dana, while a grave look overspread his face.

"Oh! not at all," said Mary, with a clear, merry laugh. "I assure you, he heartily amused every one present."

"And, no doubt, brought many a blush to your sweet face," said Mr. Dana, as he rose and took the seat beside Mary. "And," he continued, in a low voice, "cousin Saunders told me much of you; he spoke of you continually in his letters, and when he visited me lately, he made you his especial theme. I had never ceased to think of you from the moment I met you in New Orleans, and when I came and saw you so infinitely beyond all that even he had pictured you, at once I laid my heart at your feet. You may think this avowal premature, dear Mary, but in the sleepless night I passed after your last evening's divine music, I made up my mind to seize the first opportunity to tell you how much I love you. I love you, Mary! I love you sincerely! I would be all in all to you—friend, protector, cherisher, lover."

And the young girl bent her head low on her breast, while she trembled violently.

"Is there, then, *no* hope for me?" he continued, and
his voice was sad, as she gave no sign.   "Oh! speak,
Mary," he went on, "put an end to this suspense;
have you, then, no encouraging word?   Speak,.
dearest!"

"There is hope," said Mary, as, with an effort, she
raised her head, and her eyes suffused with tears,
sought his, and dropped again as quickly.   "God
and my father willing, I will be to you all you desire—
your best friend, your comforter."

He raised to his lips the hand that lay nearest
him; he would have given world to have sealed the
compact on her lips, but there was such a modest
dignity in her manner, as forbade even the thought.

The coach stopped, and as they entered the gate
and drove up to the house of Mr. Caldwell, both
countenances had so assumed their usual appearance,
that a stranger would never have supposed a tender
word had been said or listened to by either.

Mrs. Caldwell was delighted to welcome Mr. Dana,
and greeted Mary with an affectionate kiss.   Mr. Dana
silently envied Mrs. Caldwell her salutation, and
thought, "How tantalizing that ladies should kiss each
other in the presence of gentlemen!"

Mrs. Caldwell's children, three in number, came
dancing and jumping round Mary, kissing and caress-
ing her, and while Mr. Dana and their mother talked
earnestly, seemingly very much interested in the conversation, Mary could not, even in these distractions,
but realize that she had just entered a new world.
As she stepped across its threshold, a feeling of awe

mingled with the pervading sense of happiness, and the moon and the stars beamed down with holy light from its pure heaven into her calm soul.

What a change in her young life! What a sweet agitation filled her! What a heart full of rich thoughts, of new hopes, of new prayers, of delightful ambitions! Some one to live for now, some one to whose wants she could minister, whose griefs she could bind up, whose sorrows she could soothe, whose joys she could brighten by partaking them, whose happiness she might increase. And as the delicious knowledge of being beloved by him whose rich, soft tones and words fell on her ear, seemed gradually to dawn upon her, her thoughts ascended in praise and gratitude to God.

During the ride home Mr. Dana told Mary he was obliged to leave the city that afternoon, that he would come and pay his respects to Mrs. Lincoln and herself at an early hour, that he would write her immediately upon his arrival in New York, and that he would not be long absent. He prayed her to answer his letter as speedily as possible, and smiled as she half shook her head at the request, and said she was not in the habit of writing to gentlemen.

"But," said Mr. Dana, "I am sure your kindness will grant me the boon I ask, for how can I be happy without it, Mary?" and he pressed in both his the little cold hand that lay beside him.

Arrived at Mr. Lincoln's he handed Mary tenderly from the carriage, he walked up the stone-steps with her, rang the bell, declined her invitation to dinner, and as Bessie opened the door, touched his hat, and turned from the house.

Mary did not even cast a glance at his noble, re-treating figure, but hurried up to her attic room, her dear, far off room, where she could unseen, indulge her emotions. She laid aside her gloves, her summer shawl, her hat, and poured out some water to cool her hot cheeks. Calm in appearance she went down to dinner, with quiet manner spoke of the drive, and Mrs. Caldwell's pleasure at seeing Mr. Dana; she related all the winning ways of the children; it is strange that she observed them, occupied, as she was, with her own thoughts and feelings.

Early in the afternoon Mr. Dana called to tell Mrs. and Miss Lincoln good-by. He sat beside Mrs. Lincoln, wholly engrossed, as it were, in the little nothings she was telling him. He rose to take leave; he kissed his cousin, and gayly talking she preceded him to the hall; he advanced to Mary; she trembled as if she would have fallen, but she waived back his proffered embrace, and, with a sigh, he took both her hands in his, and whispered in her ear—" God bless you, my darling!" and was gone.

At tea, Mr. Lincoln did not appear to be in the best imaginable spirits. No usual flashes of wit and of humor passed between Mrs. Lincoln and himself, and Mrs. Lincoln thinking he might not be well, asked him if he had a headache. He answered no. He would have said he had a heartache, but thought silence more advisable at present.

As they rose from the table her father said to Mary:

"I wish to see you immediately *alone*, in the library."

With palpitating heart, Mary, as if she were going on to some great misery, as, indeed, she was, followed. Mr. Lincoln seated her on the sofa, and placed himself beside her. In a solemn tone he began:

"Mary, I had a visit this afternoon, at my office, from Mr. Dana. He told me he had made a declaration to you this morning, which he had reason to hope was not unacceptable. He told me he loved you— loves rather the *money* he hopes to get with you," said Mr. Lincoln, rising and marching with rapid strides across the floor. "I do not like this man; I tell you I do not like this man. I did not like him from the first moment I looked at him. My word for it, he is nothing but an adventurer, Mrs. Lincoln to the contrary notwithstanding," and Mr. Lincoln's voice grew louder. "Does he think, he a total stranger to me, to come into my house and take away my daughter. I tell you no man whose history I do not know from beginning to end, with whose disposition, whose character, I am not acquainted, even were he prince of nations, shall ever marry a daughter of mine. The insolent fellow!" and Mr. Lincoln's face grew crimson, and his eye flashed fire, and Mary paled and trembled like an aspen. "A pretty how to do, I must confess! Coming into a man's house and looking twice at his daughter, and then, forsooth, he must have the impudence to want to carry her right off, before his eyes, without even so much, as by your leave. Mrs. Lincoln ought to have known better than to have sent you away alone with him this morning. It was nothing but a scheme between them, I have n't the least doubt in the world!"

Where were Mary's beautiful dreams now? Rudely vanished, I ween; all melted away into thin air.

Mr. Lincoln grew calmer, and with a softer voice he said:

"Mary, I *hope* your affections are not enlisted in this bad cause. It is nothing but a fancy you have for this man, which will soon wear off, I am sure. Strive to forget him, my child; believe me, however cold my manner may be to you at times, and God help me, I know I am to blame, for the sake of peace and quiet, I have sacrificed your feelings; but, my dear daughter," and Mr. Lincoln sat beside his child and put his arm round her trembling frame, "your happiness is very dear to me. I should never forgive myself if I allowed you to be drawn into a snare from which you can never, *never*, escape, and which will prove your lasting sorrow." And as he laid her head on his bosom, and kissed her cheek— the first kiss of years—he said: "Promise me, Mary, that you will not listen to this suit;" and Mary said, between her sobs, her voice choked with tears—

"Father! I promise you!"

CHAPTER XVI.

In what a frame of mind Mary rose the next morning and went about her usual employments! No warm sunlight of love and joy streamed like a golden flood into the heart which was dead and heavy; no hopes danced in her young path, now overshadowed by clouds as black as the starless night. Mechanically she performed her tasks, without a sigh, without a moan, without a tear. Clouds also seemed looming up in Mrs. Lincoln's horizon. In the waking hours of the night she had labored assiduously in the cause of her friend and her step-daughter. She had vainly combatted the prejudices of Mr. Lincoln—*prejudices* she was pleased to call his evident dislike for Mr. Dana. She had declared she could not see the reason for his decided objections to the gentleman—his family was aristocratic—his health, untainted—his morals, unimpeachable—his wealth, sufficient—his character, noble and magnanimous.

But Mr. Lincoln went out after the meal in the same frame of mind as yesterday had left him in, quite as firm in his opinions, quite as unalterable in his decisions.

12

Mary kept her room at dinner, kept it all day, and could not rise the next morning because of a nervous headache, and drooped and languished thus for some time.

But on the fifth day, Gertrude sent her a note saying that she was paying a short visit to Kate Lee, and they intended spending this evening with her, and bringing Mr. Laralde with them.

She rose and dressed herself, and made a desperate effort to be cheerful. Pride came to her relief—not for the world would she have any one know the trial through which she was passing. She was very gay; her eyes sparkled, her cheeks flushed and burned as the merry laugh issued from her parted lips, and Kate and Gertrude and Mr. Laralde, all said afterward, how charming she was. After they had bade good-night, Mr. Lincoln, with gloomy countenance, handed his daughter a scaled letter, post-marked New York. She paled and reddened as her eye read the superscription, and placing it in her pocket, at the first opportunity noiselessly glided from the room. On her knees, under the gaslight, in her silent chamber, she broke the seal, and with mingled emotions of fear, of sorrow, of bliss, of misery, she began:

"MY OWN DEAR MARY:

"I arrived this evening in excellent health and spirits. The voyage was agreeable in all save the knowledge that each moment carried me farther from one who occupies all my heart. I hasten to lay again at your feet, my esteem, my love, my devotion; these, your own precious words gave me reason to believe, although unworthy, are not indifferent to you. Indeed, the little you spoke, in your maidenly reserve, revealing to me your heart was inclined toward me, filled me with inexpressible joy and gratitude. I can scarcely realize that I have gained something for which, through long years I have been seeking, the affection of a noble soul, and since I left you I begin to think better of myself. I begin to think, perhaps, I am somebody after all—for nobody that was not somebody could have won such a heart as Mary Lincoln's, and I am proud, yet humbly so, I trust before God, who can and will justly and righteously weigh us.

"And, with a heart fuller of thankfulness than it ever was before, I beseech God to infuse thy spirit into my soul, that He would make me worthy to commune with thee with confidence and without trembling—that my want of it might be supplied by thy abundance of goodness—that thy love might so purify my heart that no tear, no sigh should ever escape thee of my causing, and no regret should ever touch thee that I did not doubly share and chase away.

"The same post that bears this to you, also carries a letter from me to your father. Although Mrs. Lincoln and Mr. Caldwell have known me from my boyhood, and it would seem superfluous to refer to them; yet, Mr. Lincoln might imagine them, through old acquaintanceship, biased in my favor. I feel it due to the father of her I love that I should submit to him my plans, that I should acquaint him of my business po-

sition, my prospects, and refer him to those I have
known well in later years, for proofs of my character,
and for all he would very naturally desire to know of
the man to whom he commits so great a prize as his
child.   And I sincerely hope he will look with kindness, with approval on the sentiment which unites our
hearts.

"To hear from you very soon, my love, is my great
desire; then—with this—and this, and this *one* kiss, I
bid thee good night, and God bless thee."

Mary shed great tears of love and despair over this
letter, and folded it, after she had read it again and
again, and laid it under her pillow.

In the morning, while with haggard look she dressed,
a sudden thought seized her—with the letter in her
hand she walked straight to her mother's door, and
when Mrs. Lincoln opened it, Mary said in a low voice,
presenting the letter to her:

"Mother! read this, and give it to my father; desire
him to read it for my sake."

Back to her room she went, and paced her floor, and
laid her cheek against the cold wall, in utter wretchedness.   The letter had only aggravated her suffer-
ings.   No dinner—no supper—no breakfast—again
no dinner; nothing but a glass of cold water; and Mr.
Lincoln, in distress, walked the floor of the parlors,
with his hands clasped behind him, and suddenly
quitted the room, returning as suddenly again.   And
Mrs. Lincoln said, "That poor child up stairs, will
grieve herself to death;" and Mr. Lincoln at these
words bounded from his chair, and went out slam-

ming the door after him, and came in in a few moments, went straight up to Mrs. Lincoln, and said
abruptly :

"Go to her this moment! tell her to marry him, if
she likes. God help me, if I have been wrong, and
forgive me all the sorrow I have caused her! Tell her
to write him this moment, for I might change my mind
again. I seem to be utterly beside myself lately." Mr.
Lincoln caught up his hat and went out; Mrs. Lincoln
walked directly up stairs to the room she scarcely, if
ever, entered. Silently she approached Mary, who
sat with folded arms, and head bent down. She knelt
beside her, and said,

"Look up, my child, I have news for you, good
news for you;" and she put her arm round her, and
gently drew her up. "Your father gives his consent,
Mary, his free, willing consent, and bids you write
Mr. Dana immediately."

With a glad look, between the bright tears that
came swiftly down, Mary kissed her mother again and
again, and said,

"I know *you* are the author of this change in my
father's sentiments, dear mother, and I trust I shall
never cease to show you my gratitude for this kindness."

"Write immediately, my child, and never let Mr.
Dana know through what a struggle you have passed,"
said Mrs. Lincoln, as she quitted the chamber.

It was sometime before Mary could fully realize
the sudden change in her position, and before she
could calm herself sufficiently to write; but as soon as

she sat down, pen in hand, the words came thronging so fast that she could scarcely trace them. She wrote:

"Think not, dear friend, because I have allowed two days to elapse since your kind letter came to hand, without sending you a reply, that I do not intend to answer it at all. You know I am, unaccustomed to correspond with gentlemen, as I told you, and, therefore, it takes a little time to write with the palpitations which will, spite of me, begin with redoubled force, even at the direful *thought* of commencing my first epistle. Luckily, I am now more calm, and a truce to all nonsense, for a short time at least, while I hold communion with you.

"Let me first thank you for all your words of tenderness, as well as for these last, which I read with tears—tears of hope and gratitude—hope that I may soon again behold their author, and gratitude to the Giver of every good and perfect gift, for this last and most precious kindness—the bestowal of your love.

"Ah! will you have me blushingly and softly whisper how those words steal into my heart at all times, in all places, filling me with tumultuous and blissful throbbings? In my dreams, in the morning hour, through the day, in the society of those so short a time ago I deemed particularly agreeable, but now how changed!—yes! always those cherished words are before me—those dark eyes, so full of soul—those gentle, musical tones! Now, thou whom my soul loveth art so far away, and canst not see me tremble, I may tell thee how much I am engrossed by one all-prevailing object—how much I desire to make the whole happiness of one dear to me—that I might create for him a world of peace and joy !—how I pray that every duty may be well performed, and that I may be blessed to him, as he will be to me. Yes! I long for every virtue, every noble trait of character, every beauty of heart and mind, for your sake alone, my truest friend !

"When you see me in fault, you will chide me tenderly, will you not ? you will teach me to be all you desire, you will overlook my short-comings ; at such times, you will not cast me out from your love, but you will let me lean softly on your bosom, and look up in your face, and show me there, that though I am unworthy, still you forgive and pity me — that you still love me ! Oh ! may God guard me so well, my friend, that you may never once turn from me in coldness or dislike !

"How often, within the last week, have I thought of these words of one of my beloved authors : 'I am a vine, and require a support. Just now I feel clearer ideas of life bursting forth. I feel a higher being waking within me—a new world opens to me. Would I could wander through it, hand in hand, with one whom I could love and esteem—'

" And my heart beat gladly as something within me asked : 'Ah ! now thou hast found thy oak, hast thou not ?—thy strong support, thy life !'

" And this vine, this crooked vine, with pride and joy replies tremblingly and low : 'I have found, and will closely cling to, the oak I love !'

" Adieu, my friend, may God protect and guard you, is the prayer of,

　　　　　　 "Thine, ever,　　　　MARY."

The letter was enveloped, directed, and sealed, and Mrs. Lincoln called John to take it to the post-office as speedily as possible; nor did she breathe quite freely until he returned and said he had safely fulfilled his mission.

At dinner Mary wore a more hopeful aspect, although she was very grave. Mr. Lincoln seemed more cheerful, and even began, before the meal was ended, to joke, according to custom, with his wife.

A few days after came another missive for Mary, which, in the obscurity of her chamber, no eye but God's and hers saw.

It was this:

" Oh, Mary, dearest! the joy thy dear letter gave me is beyond expression of the pen—tongue and the eye, love, would fail, even wert thou present, in conveying to thee its depth—its utter fullness!

" 'When you see me in fault.' Yes, dear, dear Mary, you shall lay your head gently on my bosom—look up in my face—tell me how dearly you love me, and tell me, if I do so and so, I shall grieve you—such a reproof, dearest, I much fear, I shall deserve at thy hands—but such chiding once, God grant, may be enough—I were a stone else. Yes! Mary, 'tis to thee I shall look for rebuke, for *I* only shall do wrong—for counsel and direction in my duty, for *I* only shall be weak, and require support, and thou wilt give it me in love, dearest, wilt thou not? But nay, my own dear wife, I shall not be weak—with thy support, I shall be strong—with Heaven's blessing, we shall both be strong, both to do His will and to bear cheerfully the burdens He may cast upon us.

" I *will* be thy oak, dear Mary, and thou shalt be my vine — ' crooked vine! ' My life, if thou wert not crooked, how couldst thou have so twined thyself about my very heart!—tell me that!—how could that vine, in its upward growth, creep into every crevice—wind around every knot of so gnarled a trunk?

" It is now nine o'clock at night—perhaps you are asleep ; no, perhaps you are at the piano, practicing some little home-song you mean to sing to me when the toils of day are over ; perhaps sitting by yourself, and asking your heart if I shall always love thee as tenderly as now. Do not doubt it, dearest, or perhaps—and God grant it—you are on your knees beseeching Him to raise me up to being worthy of your love—that He would touch my soul with a spark from the altar of the living God—soften my heart to a full perception of my unworthiness of his unnumbered mercies. It is this consummation, dear companion of my future years, that I look for at thy hands.

" May what I write find thee happy, my own love, and make thee more so ; and it will, if the assurance can do so of the devoted affection of one so unworthy as I am.

13

"Yet once again, accept my vows! I will hang upon thy lips moving in prayer with fervent devotion—in counsel with humility—in love, with stronger love for thee, and with deep-felt gratitude to Him who has bestowed upon me so precious a blessing. God be with thee!

"Now, and ever, and only thine,

"WM. DANA."

CHAPTER XVII.

A few days after the reception of this letter, which brought a tide of happiness to Mary Lincoln, Caroline Thomas sent her a note, one morning, requesting her to accompany her to call upon some young ladies, strangers, who were visiting a mutual friend.

Mary returned quite early, and as Bessie opened the front door, at her summons, she said to her:

"Bessie, is it late?"

"No, Miss Mary," answered Bessie, "it will be more than an hour before dinner time."

"Is mother at home yet?" asked Mary.

"No, Miss Mary, not yet," was the response.

Mary ascended to her room, took off her gloves and her summer mantle and bonnet, which, as usual, she carefully laid away in their several places, changed her street dress for her home afternoon dress, and, thinking she had some time to practice, took her way softly down stairs. She entered the back parlor and opened the piano, but hearing the rustling of paper in the sitting-room, she thought it was strange her father should be at home so much earlier than his

custom. She stepped to the glass door between the
rooms, and at a glance she saw it was another, and
not her father who sat there.   A cry of glad surprise
burst from her lips, and in a moment she was folded
in the tender embrace of her lover.

"I did not know you were here," said Mary; "how
stupid in Bessie not to tell me! how lucky that I did
not spend the rest of the morning in my chamber!"

"And so have lost my agreeable society," said Mr.
Dana, smiling.

"And to have lost an hour, never again to be recalled," said Mary, without looking up.

Mr. Dana led her into the back parlor, placed her
on the sofa, and seated himself beside her.   And with
her head pillowed on his bosom he bent over her, and
in a low voice, he thanked her again for her love, for
her letter.   He told her of his journey, of the friends
he had met, of his sister-in-law (the widow of his
beloved brother—his last surviving brother); and as
he spoke he drew from his pocket a dainty-looking
little note, which Mrs. Dana had sent to Mary, and
which Mary received consciously and blushingly.   He
drew from another pocket a small box, and taking
from it a magnificent diamond ring, he placed it on
Mary's finger, while he breathed again his words of
love.   Then he told her his plans—that he must return, on the morrow, to New Orleans; that he hoped
she would consent that he might come, in six weeks
from that day, and claim her as his bride; for by that
time all trace of fever would have disappeared from

his southern home. And when Mary spoke of the danger and risk he ran in going back, at this season, and wished he could stay longer, he smiled and said, "sixteen years spent in the south had acclimated him, and therefore he had no fears;" and when he pointed to the bald spot on his head, and to his crisp hair, and said those were the effects of yellow-fever, Mary involuntarily shuddered; and when he said he was but a wreck of former years, Mary thought, "then he must indeed have been divine!"

When Mary heard the click of her father's door-key in the lock, as he entered accompanied by her mother, she could not but feel a little anxious as to how he would receive Mr. Dana. But her perturbations were soon quieted, for Mr. Lincoln welcomed his intended son-in-law with great kindness, and even warmth of manner.

At dinner, Mr. Dana's narration and description of incidents and scenes, witnessed in his travels, for he had seen much of the world; his unobtrusive attention to the comfort and desires of those present; the tenderness his tone involuntarily assumed when he addressed Mary; the polish and grace of his manner, called forth, in addition to her love and esteem, sentiments of pride and of admiration.

After dinner, Mr. Lincoln lingered an hour, and then invited Mr. Dana to walk with him. Mary felt a pang as the door closed upon her lover, for she could not bear the thought of losing a moment of his short stay with them.

The gentlemen returned some time before " tea,"

which slight repast was served by Bessie on two silver
waiters, placed on small tables in the sitting-room.

Mary poured out a cup of coffee for her mother, for
her father, and slightly trembled as she performed the
same office for Mr. Dana, who stood near her, and
whose eyes, she *knew*, were fixed upon her. With a
blush she gave, and with a smile he received, the cup
of fragrant Mocha.

As twilight came on, the little circle withdrew to
the front parlor and sat awhile in the deepening
shadows.   Bessie lighted a jet of gas in the sitting-
room, which light, from where they sat, looked like a
star.   The full moon streamed in at the open windows,
and the breath of the evening air was cool and delightful.

Mr. Dana rose, and approaching Mary, asked, with
Mr. and Mrs. Lincoln's permission, if she would not
act as guide, this evening, and show him some parts
of the city which he had never seen, as all the streets
were new to him except some of the principal business
thoroughfares.   Mr. and Mrs. Lincoln cheerfully ac-
· quiesced, and Mary replied that she would be happy
to escort him, and so went to get her shawl and bonnet.

It was indeed a lovely night, and much pleasanter
to be out, than within doors.   One half the street was
in deep shadow, the other half in full light.   The long
lines of trees, edging both sidewalks, had not yet lost
a leaf—were not yet tinged with autumn hues.   In
the open doors and on the stone steps of contiguous
dwellings, sat groups of young persons merrily chat-

ting, while others, young maidens with arms intertwined, promenaded up and down the stone pavement. Every now and then a low, joyous laugh came floating over the night air.

Mary felt, to the utmost, the beauty of the hour, and would have been supremely happy, leaning on the arm of her lover, had she not so dreaded the parting which she knew must come speedily. Ah! are there not always thorns with the roses?

Soon our friends turned into a broad, beautiful street, the handsomest in the city. Here the houses stood up high, surrounded and decorated by their garden-spots. In one of these magnificent dwellings lived Caroline Thomas. Mary spoke of her, and of Kate Lee, and of Gertrude. She expatiated rapturously upon Gertrude's beauty, and noble character, and wished Mr. Dana could have remained longer, so that he might have met her.

"And is that the only reason, dearest, you would have me stay?" said Mr. Dana, as he bent a look upon his companion.

"I have more selfish reasons for desiring you to remain longer," said Mary. "The thought of your absence fills me with grief;" and her face did indeed look very sad, in the pale moonlight. A pang shot through her companion's heart as he thought of the many months that would intervene before he should see her again. It was to tell her this that he had invited her to walk with him this evening. During the afternoon he had laid his plans before Mr. Lincoln; he had asked that the hand of Mary might soon

be his; to which request Mr. Lincoln had most decidedly objected.   As Mary listened, her heart fell,
and a thousand forebodings possessed her.

"Mr. Lincoln does not approve of short engage-
ments," said Mr. Dana, " and he will not consent to
his daughter's marriage in less than a year from *this*
time.   The reasons he gives for a postponement of
your nuptials are, your youth, Mary," continued Mr.
Dana, " and a course of uncompleted study, on which
he has set his heart.   I will not speak of my great
disappointment.   I will not tell you how my busy
mind has been at work sweetly picturing happy hours
near at hand, in our quiet home with my loved Mary.
I will not speak of the pride and joy with which I
looked forward to the speedy consummation of my
hope.   I will not tell you how the thought of this
hope deferred maketh my heart sick.   At the same
time, I can not but acknowledge the superior wisdom
of Mr. Lincoln, and bow to it with meek submission."

" I am sure, my dear father intends all for the best,"
said Mary, with a tearful smile, " and I shall have
longer time to make myself more worthy of you.   I
shall have more time to learn to be a good housekeeper; to study everything I can, that will increase
your comfort and your happiness.   Believe me, I shall
not be idle."

Mr. Dana smiled thoughtfully, as he drew Mary's
arm more tenderly within his own, and said, " You are
much too good for me *now*, dear Mary, and I am not
half worthy of you."

When they entered the parlors, their walk ended, Mrs. Lincoln said :

"Caroline Thomas, Kate Lee, and Gertrude, have just gone, Mary; they were here with Mr. Laralde and two strangers, gentlemen. They all expressed much disappointment at not seeing you; and Mr. Laralde said, he should do himself the honor of calling again soon."

"I am sorry not to have seen them," said Mary, "especially Gertrude ; will she go home to-morrow, mother ? "

"I think not," said Mrs. Lincoln," at least, if she consults Mr. Laralde's pleasure. I am sure she will remain longer, for he protested against so short a visit."

"And who is Mr. Laralde ?" said Mr. Dana, seating himself near Mary ; "is he a *fascinating* gentleman ? "

"One would think so," said Mrs. Lincoln, with a twinkle of the eye, "to see all the attentions these young ladies bestow upon him; indeed, sometimes I think our Mary, here, is hardly proof against his charms."

"Oh, mother! how can you talk so ?" said Mary, really quite annoyed; "you have repeatedly heard me say, that I do not even admire him, and I wonder the girls can find anything in his appearance or manners so attractive as to make him the theme of even a five minutes' conversation ! "

"Will you describe him, Mary," asked Mr. Dana, while he twirled a little uneasily his moustache.

"He is very tall," said Mary, "has a very clear complexion, very light hair, very blue eyes, very white teeth, very high forehead, and would look decidedly intellectual, if he wore spectacles. He is an ex-professor of mathematics in some college at the East, and has come to our city to exercise his talents in the profession of the law. To me, he is superlatively insipid, superlatively awkward, superlatively uninteresting—in short, I have no patience with him. He is equally devoted to Gertrude and Kate Lee; indeed, I think he has a *very* tender feeling for Gertrude, for when she visits us he spends every evening here, and stays so late, that I can scarcely refrain from showing him that I am tired to death of him, and so sleepy that I can scarcely keep awake."

"He is equally devoted to Mary, I can assure you, cousin William," said Mrs. Lincoln, with a merry laugh, as she arose to say good-night; "I advise you, before you go, to lay your commands upon this young lady."

"Mr. Dana may rest assured that I shall never, in thought or deed, do anything that would cause him a moment's unrest or pain," said Mary, as she too rose to bid her mother good-night.

Mr. Dana lingered, dreading to say what Mary so dreaded to hear—farewell! It was a long absence to look forward to—an absence of nearly a year—and in that time what circumstances might arise to change Mary's feelings, in regard to him, was a question Mrs. Lincoln's *plaisanterie* had suggested. Would she be true to him? he asked himself, as he looked into the

face whose soft cheek rested lovingly and confidingly
on his bosom. He could not see the liquid eyes,
veiled as they were by their drooping lids ; but there
was in the countenance such truth, such strength of
purpose, even such divinity, that all doubts vanished
on the instant. Could he have looked into that pure
heart, from which fervent prayers were now ascending
for him—prayers for his safety, for his health, for his
happiness, for his prosperity, he would have been
ashamed and humiliated that he had, even for an instant, indulged in such doubts—in such weakness.

CHAPTER XVIII.

IN the first weary watches of the night, Mary gave way to regret at the separation from her lover ; but, at last, she philosophically concluded to banish useless repinings, and to strive to busy herself so effectually that time should pass quickly—pass, as she had told him, in endeavors to make herself more worthy of his choice, to make herself a proficient in everything that should add to his future comfort — add to his esteem for her. Therefore, after again commending him to the protection and love of Him who watches over all, pleased at the thought of striving to make herself a "perfect woman," she spent her last wakeful hour in plans for pursuing more diligently her duties, her reading—of cultivating more assiduously her accomplishments, thus fitting herself to be a partner in his joys and intellectual pleasures, as well as a sympathizer in sorrow—a guardian angel in the dark hours which come to every one in this weary world of ours, as well as the "cherished companion of his future years." With these plans uppermost, she descended to breakfast, wearing a cheerful aspect, which both pleased and agreeably surprised her father and mother. An hour later, as she stood at the breakfast table carefully washing the silver and glass, with these plans still uppermost, she said to Mrs. Lincoln:

"Mother, what do you think of my learning to cook? If you are willing, I will undertake to prepare and cook the dinner, once every week, if you think best."

" I think it an excellent suggestion, my dear," said Mrs. Lincoln; " you know it is a part of my theory, that the culinary art should be introduced into the education of every young lady. I never could understand why so many women, otherwise sensible, should have such an infinite disgust for everything pertaining to the kitchen, and why they should boast that their feet never stepped within its unknown precincts. Surely, knowledge which adds so much to the comfort, to the health—yes, to the *happiness* of a family, ought not to be considered despicable. In my eyes, the woman who knows how to conduct well her household, how to manage, with prudence, with economy, with judgment, is quite as deserving of a crown, as she who excels in literature, in art, or in science. In this country, where we are so subject to the caprices of servants, how necessary that all women who would be rid of a thousand perplexities and annoyances, so wearing and tearing to the disposition, should be prepared for this and every other emergency! A woman who knows how to prepare a meal excellently, gracefully and expeditiously may be sure not only of the gratitude of her husband, but of the esteem of her domestics. I so often think," continued Mrs. Lincoln, " of a young intimate friend of mine, who married under auspicious circumstances, and with brilliant prospects, the man of her choice. Immediately after the ceremony she quitted her native city and the city of her parents, for her husband's home, where already prepared for her was a handsome house, furnished with every luxury.

" With bright anticipations of happiness, she undertook the duties, which, through ignorance, she was wholly incompetent to perform. Tenderly reared by a mother, whose whole desire had been to see her daughters thoroughly educated, and elegantly accomplished, she was an utter stranger to all matters pertaining to housekeeping. How often, in after years, with a grave face, she related to me the trials, the bitternesses, the heart-burnings, the mortifications of her first years of married life ! how often her husband, who had been a devoted lover, rose with a moody countenance, and a frigid manner, from his untasted meal, and went to a hotel or an eating-house to satisfy the cravings of hunger ! She would recall her ineffectual attempts to direct and train her ignorant servants—her vain efforts to make a stupid cook understand what was far beyond her own comprehension.

" Sometimes, with a merry laugh, she would tell me how she had found herself obliged to resort to duplicity in order not to be despised by those under her sway; how she would run stealthily to her cook-book to study by heart the recipe, which she pretended to know practically—and as stealthily hide her book when she heard on the stairs the footsteps of Bridget, who came for fuller directions ; and then her husband's disgust when the much-talked-of dish would appear upon the table, perhaps lacking one of the principal ingredients, absolutely spoiled through her lack of memory, or inattention."

" I suppose there are hundreds of similar cases," said Mary.

" No doubt," said Mrs. Lincoln.

" Perhaps, mother," said Mary, " this is a suitable time for me to tell you, what I have long intended doing, how much I appreciate the lessons you have already given me in household matters. They were very irksome at first, I candidly acknowledge, but now they interest and please me, and I feel that I have already turned over one great page in the new book you opened for my instruction. I feel that you have taught me neatness, promptness, method and order, and how to use my time to the best advantage ; and I thank you very heartily, dear mother, for all your care."

" Do not give me more credit than I deserve, my child," said Mrs. Lincoln, " you certainly required no lessons in neatness and order. I found you all that I could desire in that respect. But," continued Mrs. Lincoln, " this new study, of which we are talking, will occupy much of your time—one entire morning in the week—and that with your hours of reading to me, with you Latin, and Mr. Droune's reading, will leave you very little leisure."

" I am very willing, mother," said Mary, " to deny

myself, during these hours to visitors, to all except to
Gertrude, who I am sure should she be here on my
' cooking day,' will be quite willing to give me instruction, as she is herself an accomplished housekeeper."

"If we can put any faith in signs," said Mrs. Lincoln, "before long, Gertrude will have a house of her
own to direct."

"I am sure she will never leave her father," said
Mary. "Mr. Laralde, or whoever may be the favored
one, will find himself obliged to live with Mr. Clifford.
In my eyes, Gertrude's filial devotion is one of her
greatest charms."

"It is, indeed, a lovely trait of character, and one
that any man must appreciate, particularly such a man
as Mr. Laralde," said Mrs. Lincoln, as she folded her
work, and laid it in her little work-basket.

"I think he is sensible of this quality of my dear
Gertrude, and admires it as much as he does all her
virtues and all her nobleness," said Mary.

"I am quite sure of it," replied Mrs. Lincoln, as
she quitted the room, and gently closed the door after
her.

CHAPTER XIX.

THIS winter was the happiest Mary had ever known. It is true, there were moments when her longing to see her absent lover was almost too great to be borne, when it seemed as if the time for his return would never draw near — moments of despondency which, however, her gay, brave heart fought against, and took strength and hope again to wait patiently for his return.

After Mr. Dana's arrival in New Orleans, Mary regularly received from him letters, books, the latest music, and sometimes birds and tropical plants, so that in a short time she might have set up an aviary, and might, with her rare plants, have filled a small greenhouse. With what delight she tended her birds and plants, and how they prospered under her care; the little feathered songsters came at her bidding, and she sometimes smiled as she thought it was the soft airs she warbled that made the buds and blossoms spring so joyously to life. Mr. Dana's letters were a great consolation in his absence, and it was an equal solace to Mary to answer them. Here she could pour out her heart; here she could express its warmth for him,

14

so much better than she could if he were present and
looking at her.　Here she told him all her plans, her
occupations; she discussed with him the last new
music; she criticized the latest book, and spoke of different subjects brought to notice in the readings of
Mr. Droune; she told him she was still declining and
conjugating Latin words, and that her interest in the
language was constantly increasing.　A friend had
lately sent her 'Rossini's Stabat Mater.'　She had
never before heard it.　It had so thrilled her, so
touched her, that she could not forbear writing to her
lover of its effect upon her.　She said:

"Every time I listen to those sublime harmonies,
as they swell in grandeur on my ear, and die away in
plaintive melody, I stand with the 'Mater Dolorosa'
before the cross, where hangs the only Son of God.
Waves of sorrow roll over my soul, as I contemplate
the agony, the anguish of the mother of the Man of
grief.　In His gaping wounds I behold my sins, in His
divine countenance, in His drooping head from which
life has fled, I see all the compassion, all the forgive-
ness of the Godhead; I understand in all its depth,
in all its fullness, that love with which *He'so* loved the
world, as to give His only begotten Son a ransom for
my wickedness.　And how great it seems! how deeper
than scarlet! how blacker than midnight! Can anything deliver me of this stupendous burden?

"And then a sweet low voice steals like heavenly
music on my ear: 'Come unto me all ye that labor,
and are heavy laden, and I will give you rest—though
your sins be as scarlet, I will make them whiter than

snow.' And as I look at the dripping blood shed for
me, I pray for grace to live a new life, to glorify my
risen Savior, to devote my energies to Him—my love,
my all. I pray, my friend, that hand in hand we may
walk adown the vale of years, rejoicing in the light of
His divine love, fighting the good fight, and winning
at last the crown."

Accidently Gertrude had heard Mr. Droune read and
explain to Mrs. Lincoln and Mary, and was so delighted with the man, and his manner of communicating his extensive information, that she requested to
be permitted to join his little class; so enthusiastic
was she in her expression of delight at the knowledge
gained in these readings, that Mrs. Day, also as an
especial favor, desired to make one of the number,
which was soon afterward increased by other agreeable acquaintances, and even Mr. Clifford dropped in
occasionally. Each member determined resolutely not
to be ashamed of her ignorance, but to ask as many
questions as she wished on every subject which should
be presented.

Many discussions arose, sometimes very extensive,
very animated, and certainly very improving.

The history of Italy was the theme under contemplation, a theme so broad, so grand, that it promised
to occupy many afternoons. Its poets, its historians,
its munificent patrons of art, its magnificent architec-
ture, its painters, its sculptors, its musicians, all came
in for a share of notice—Petrarch, Tasso, Dante, Ari-
osto, Metastasio, and other poets were discussed, and

Mr. Droune read parts of each to his auditors. Mary was charmed beyond expression with the Gerusalemme, with its noble characters, its exquisite descriptions, its beautiful thoughts, and the harmonious rythm of its delightful translation, and wrote to Mr. Dana begging him to read it if he had not previously done so.

After one of these afternoons, which had been unusually interesting and spirited, made so by the sketches of the lives of some of the most famous Italian painters, and their world-renowned pictures, drawn with vividness and grace by Mr. Clifford, Gertrude and Mary drew their chairs close up beside Mrs. Lincoln, and near the bright sitting-room fire, and full of the delightful hours they had just passed, thus continued with enthusiasm to discuss different works of art they had seen.

Mrs. Lincoln had been unusually brilliant, to-day; a slight feeling of envy mingled with Mary's admiration of her mother, and with this emotion dominant she said rather abruptly, as Gertrude's last words died on the ear:

"Mother, will you not teach me the art of *conversation?* It is an accomplishment I ardently admire, and long to possess, but how to attain it, how to make myself a proficient, is an enigma I can not solve. In vain, in my search after knowledge, have I read all the chapters on conversation which have fallen into my hands—and I can glean nothing, nothing whatever, to enlighten my groping mind. I am told, firstly, that reading enriches the mind, but that conversation polishes it; all which must be evident to the most unenlightened person ; and, secondly, I am taught that to make myself agreeable to those who talk, I must preserve a fascinating silence, that is, I must charm the speaker by listening to him with my whole soul in my eyes—with an expression of the most intense admiration for him and for what he is saying. Is conversation a talent that is born with us, or is it an acquired possession ; what do you think on the subject, dear mother ?"

"I think conversation is decidedly a talent," said Mrs. Lincoln, while her two young hearers listened attentively. "I have seen young children who uttered the most curious thoughts in the most clear, in the most graphic way, and again with a flow of language perfectly wonderful. Do you remember what Cowper says on the subject ?

> ' Though *conversation*, in its better part,
> May be esteemed a gift and not an art,
> Yet much depends, as in the tiller's toil,
> On culture, and the sowing of the soil.'

"We may cite Madame De Staël as an example of one on whom the gift of conversation was bestowed by nature, although I suppose, as Cowper says, this gift was cultivated and developed by the circumstances of her birth, her education, her *entourage*.

"I am also of the opinion that conversation may be acquired, as well as any other habit which we heartily desire. One of my maxims is, where there is a will there's a way, and when there is a strong determination to succeed in any attempt, we are sure to accomplish our object, or in the sententious style of our own Emerson: 'Our prayers are prophets. There must be fidelity, there must be adherance.' Again, in speaking of the art itself, he says: 'There is no book and no pleasure in life comparable to it.' And again: 'In excited conversation, we have glimpses of the universe, hints of power, native to the soul, far-darting lights and shadows of an Andes landscape, such as we can hardly attain in lone meditation. Here are oracles, sometimes profusely given, to which the memory goes back in barren hours.'"

"How great," said Mrs. Lincoln, "is the contrast between two men, both extremely cultivated, but of whom, one alone has developed this delightful gift. I have seen those whose conversation might have enriched and charmed the most refined circles, sit with closed mouth, while I knew that mighty thoughts were passing through their brain, and I nervously hoped each moment might give birth to their soul music. I have seen these for an instant forget themselves, and pour forth such rapid, massive ideas and phrases, as to thrill and enrupture their hearers; then, disconcerted, as if suddenly awakened by the sound of their own voice, with embarrassment, relapse into the most profound silence. I sit in the presence of such superior, uncommunicative wisdom, regretting that it can not be shared, almost indignant that it has not the power of bringing its treasures to light and life."

"It is surely a duty, then," said Mary, "that people who know a great deal of what is good and beautiful should not conceal it, should not hide it away, but should share it with those who would equally enjoy it."

"I am certainly of that opinion," said Mrs. Lincoln.

"*I* am so exceedingly *timid*," said Mary, "that I fear I shall never succeed."

"*Presence of mind* is a necessary requisite," replied Mrs. Lincoln. "Do you remember, Mary, those words of Johnson?"

"There must, in the first place, be *knowledge*—there must be materials; in the second place, there must be a command of words; in the third place, there must be imagination, to place things in such views as they are not commonly seen in; and in the fourth place, there must be *presence of mind*, and a resolution that is not to be overcome by failures: this last is an essential requisite; for want of it many people do not excel in conversation; and," continued Mrs. Lincoln, "I recall what Mrs. Jameson says on the matter, which is very pretty, but I do not know that her remarks contain any hints which the youthful pupil may seize upon, and from which he or she may derive instruction.

"Conversation may be compared to a lyre with seven chords, philosophy, art, poetry, politics, love, scandal, and the weather. There are some professors who, like Paganini, can discourse most eloquent music upon one string only, and some who can grasp the whole instrument, and, with a master's hand, sound it from the bottom to the top of its compass.

"And let us listen, now, to Miss Hannah More's

thoughts on this valuable accomplishment: 'Books alone will never form the character. Mere reading rather tends to make a pedantic, than an accomplished person. It is *conversation* which must unfold, enlarge and apply the use of books. Without that familiar comment on what is read, which will make a most important part of the intercourse between the pupil and the society around him, mere reading might not only fill the mind with fallacious models of character, and false maxims of life. It is conversation which must develop what is obscure, raise what is low, correct what is defective, qualify what is exaggerated, and gently and almost insensibly raise the understanding, form the heart, and fix the taste; and by giving just proportions to the mind, teach it the power of just appreciation, draw it to adopt what is reasonable, to love what is good, to taste what is pure, and to imitate what is elegant.'

"When I was young," continued Mrs. Lincoln, "and first directed my thoughts to the subject, I used to cut out pieces of poetry and of prose—any beautiful sentiment or description that pleased me, and pin the same on my pincushion, or fasten it to my wall, near my dressing-table, so that when making my toilet the words would be constantly before me. It was surprising how many ideas, how many expressions and phrases this practice gave me, in the course of a year; beside, it strengthened and enlarged my memory. How delightful to always carry in our hearts pictures drawn by the great and good of all ages! This habit certainly not only keeps alive ima-

gination, assists meditation, but strips our monotonous, every-day life of its ennui—the listlessness
which otherwise might beset us. I was once told by
a gentleman of superior attainments, who was intimate with a lady of whom you have both heard—a
lady who is distinguished not only as a writer but as
a conversationalist, and who, fame says, can entertain
delightfully as many as thirty gentlemen at the same
time, that it was by this process that she had arrived
at her present perfection. He told me he had known
her to deny herself, for whole days, to visitors (that
was before she was as famous as she is now) ; to shut
herself in her own room, and study quotations from different authors, for the express purpose of shining in
society, in these borrowed plumes. The gentlemen
thought it a very feminine way of winning a name."

" Then, with steady patience and perseverance,
those wonderful virtues, any one, even the most modest, I suppose, may hope at some far distant day, to
excel in this undertaking as well as all others," said
Mary, as Gertrude and herself rose to put on their
wrappings, preparatory to taking a brisk walk before
tea.

15

CHAPTER XX.

⸢ MRS. LINCOLN'S cook, Susan, had been ailing for some time, and at last, her disease so got the better of her, as to force her to give up work entirely, and be placed upon the sick list. Bessie endeavored to fill her place, while a new chambermaid was installed, pro tem., in Bessie's office; but Bessie was not expert en matière culinaire, and Mary thought it a favorable time to test her new accomplishments, as well as to add a little to their store.

The cook-book was once again drawn from its sequestered corner, and its pages well conned in search of new recipes; different ingredients were compounded, heterogeneous mixtures were massed together, many experiments were ·tried, always resulting in something to Mary's extreme satisfaction; for she was now so experienced a cuisinière that she could combine materials in such a manner as to be always highly commendable to the taste even of the most decided epicure. She found judgment, care, and attention necessary qualities in her new capacity.

What delicious soups! what astonishing desserts, of every variety, made their appearance every day upon the table. Charlottes of all kinds, meringues, puffs, puddings, plain and otherwise, filling Mr. Lincoln with wonder. But Mary had not yet made bread, and as she was very anxious to learn, her mother concluded to give her the necessary instruction.

Behold Mrs. Lincoln, then, one morning in the kitchen, at the snow-white table, her curls pushed back under a delicate lace cap, worn for the occasion, her sleeves rolled up and pinned to the shoulders of her dress, and a large, smooth, white apron tied around her waist, her dimpled hands dipped into the flour, scarcely whiter than they. Could Mr. Lincoln have seen his wife thus metamorphosed, his regard and admiration would even have been heightened, had such a thing been possible. Mary stood by, deeply interested in the process. Mrs. Lincoln poured the white, home-made yeast into the deep hollow she had made with her pretty hands—mingled, afterward, the warm milk and water she also proceeded to pour into the aforesaid scooped-out center, then began to mix and knead away with so hearty a will, and yet so gracefully, as made Mary laughingly exclaim:

"Why, mother! this exercise is quite as good as Mrs. Barton's gymnastics."

"Yes!" said Mrs. Lincoln, as her cheeks grew rosy, and she stopped a moment to rest her tired arms, long unused to such labor. Suddenly she exclaimed:

"Oh, Bessie! where is the salt? surely I have forgotten it. It is very singular that so necessary an ingredient shall have slipped me, particularly as early reminiscences ought to have enforced it upon my memory."

"Yes!" replied Mary, "you excite my curiosity, mamma, will you not gratify it?"

"It is interesting to myself only, and merely as a recollection of my youth; but I will tell you—perhaps it will help to remind you always of what I happened so nearly to forget," said Mrs. Lincoln, with a smile. "I once had a lovely young cousin, Alice Peabody by name," continued Mrs. Lincoln, whose mother was a most careless, miserable housekeeper. Changing servants continually, there were generally in the house murmurs, complaints and discomfort. For months in the family, during the time of which I speak, no bread, fit to be eaten, had made its appearance on the table, and Alice Peabody, in despair, silently concluded, for the sake of those who gathered round the family board, that such a state of affairs should go on no longer: that *she* would learn the art, and so teach the otherwise good cook. There was a mystery about this individual; bread, of which Mrs. Peabody complained bitterly, but which she made no effort to unravel, none but abominable black loaves came out of the oven on baking-days, and the waste of flour in the family was excessive and really frightful.

"One evening, about that time, a party of young ladies and gentlemen, myself included, were going to visit a favorite aunt of Alice and mine—Mrs. Barry— a splendid woman and an admirable cook and mena- gère. Alice determined she would seize this oppor- tunity to gain the coveted knowledge. She watched her time, then, when aunt Barry was alone for a moment, and seated herself on a footstool at her feet.

"'Dear auntie,'" she whispered, as she looked up inquiringly into the face bent lovingly down upon her, 'do, please, tell me how to make bread—indeed, I must learn.'

"'With pleasure, my darling,'" replied Mrs. Barry; 'I will tell you all I know of the subject. I will teach you practically, if you choose, to make all sorts of bread, and in all the various ways.'

"'Give me one simple recipe to-night, if you will, aunt. I wish to put it in practice at the earliest opportunity,' said Alice.

"At that moment a young gentleman, who looked on my cousin with admiring eyes, approached and took a chair at aunt Barry's side, while the latter proceeded to repeat the very simple directions.

"But now the clamors of the young folks began to arise, as they called out from all quarters of the rooms for Alice Peabody. No one played dances and quadrilles so delightfully as Alice, and her name was repeated louder and louder, as she was discovered in the little group. As a gentleman approached to lead her to the piano, Mr. Goddard, who kept his seat by aunt Barry, called out: 'Do not forget the salt, Miss Alice, pray, do not forget the salt.' 'Dear me,' said our good aunt, "I am very stupid, surely, to forget so important an item.' Every one present seemed, for a time, so lost in curiosity, as to cease to remember their ardent desire to dance. 'Do not forget the salt, Miss Alice,' rang in her ears merrily, as she seated herself at the piano and drowned the noisy voices in a dashing polka.

"Alice afterward told me that, on the following morning, when the cook prepared to mix her bread, she stood beside her, aunt Barry's directions at the tip of her tongue, and was not a little startled to find that, after the yeast was put into the flour, the sponge was to be stirred up with *boiling* water.

"'Good gracious!' Kate, screamed Alice, holding the pitcher of hot water by main force, 'surely you don't mix the dough with *boiling* water?'

"'Oh yes, miss,' replied Kate, 'always.'

"'Then,' said Alice, 'I have found out the secret of your innumerable failures.'

"It is not necessary to say," continued Mrs. Lincoln, that ever afterward, cook Kate prided herself especially upon the delicious bread which invariably made its appearance on aunt Peabody's table."

"I came to the conclusion, some months ago," said Mary, "that it requires knowledge, memory, as well as a good share of intellect, to arrive at perfection in this branch of domestic science—I mean the culinary department."

CHAPTER XXI.

THE spring opened delightfully. Mary not only welcomed this season as an agreeable change from the dark, rainy winter days just passed, and a pleasant contrast to them, but as a harbinger of the time which was to restore to her her lover. His letters now, too, breathed a hope of that meeting to which both looked forward with fond longing.

In the latter days of May, Mary went to make her usual spring visit at Mr. Clifford's. Always a lover of the country, she never remembered to have enjoyed it so much before. She wandered, in an ecstasy of happiness, by beds of superb roses of every variety, of every hue, of every shape, and of exquisite fragrance; she inhaled the odor of rare carnations, of sweet-scented lilies, of the richly blooming peony. She culled beautiful sweet flowers from their stems; she arranged different varieties, different colors together, to try their effect; the admirable white peony and dainty, sweet yellow lilies with a lovely tender-leafed purple blossom unknown; she placed white and yellow roses together; white and pink; crimson and white, mingling with them the delicate sweet alyssum, she decorated the house above and below, and while Mr. Clifford and Gertrude both smiled and enjoyed her delight, she sat in arbors covered with the sweet-scented clematis and the fragrant woodbine, and drank in their intoxicating perfumes: she lingered to watch the elegant Wistaria, and its graceful pendant purple blossoms, drooping from and around the pillars of the marble portico. With Gertrude she tended flower-beds, and she grouped and set out tender summer-plants; she paid visits to the kitchen garden, to the poultry yard, she counted and fed the young chickens, she gathered from nests in the chicken-house, from nests under trees, under bushes, hidden away under brush-heaps, concealed in all imaginable places, warm, fresh, white eggs— she watched the ripening strawberries, plucked May cherries; in short, she took a deep interest in *all* her friend's occupations.

They went often to see Mrs. Day, and sometimes called upon other neighbors, or took long, pleasant country walks, or with their books sought Gertrude's quiet, secluded nook on the banks of the not far distant stream. Here, reclining on the soft, rich sward, with Gertrude's arm around her, she listened to the clear, harmonious tones of that voice very dear to her, looking ever and anon into the heavenly face, whose beauty at such times seemed to Mary Lincoln resplendent, and dreaming dreams of him so far away, him of whom she never spoke save to her mother, him of whom she longed to tell her friend, but could not, for the blush and the secret shrinking which forbade her

to expose her heart, even to Gertrude. Mary sometimes felt, as she listened to the thoughts and feelings
of her companion, as if in her own reticence she was
playing false—but, dear Mary, are there no hopes, no
emotions in Gertrude's heart which are carefully
guarded even from thy loving gaze?

Summer came—July passed—and August brought
Mr. Dana—August brought him, fresh, happy, hopeful, and found Mary, bright, happy, and even gay.

He arrived very early in the morning. The front
hall door was open, and he walked in unannounced.
Mary went into the back parlor, unconscious of his
presence, and almost before she saw him she was
clasped in his loving arms.

In that quiet home, before breakfast, he told her
all his plans—his business demanded his immediate
presence in New York, but he would return in two
weeks, at least, and then, after the marriage, which
be begged would take place at that time, they would
travel to New York, or in any other direction which
she most preferred.

Mary trembled at the thought of this great change
in her life; she had been so happy in his love, and in
the performance of her duties, that to speak truly, she
had scarcely dwelt at all upon what had always seemed
to her a far-off event. Now, the idea of being brought
so near to this new, this untried world, rather startled her. The thought of quitting a home which was
now really dear to her, of leaving her father, all her
associations, of thenceforward occupying a different
relation to them, of consigning her happiness, *herself*,

to one who was yet comparatively a stranger, although
there was no choice in her affections between one and
the other, although she gave them all up to follow the
fortunes and the fate of one doubly dear to her—the
fate of one in whom she placed implicit confidence—
one more to her than friends, than home, dearer even—
oh Mary Lincoln—than the revered father of her
youthful years, than the loved father of her later life,
was indeed a sad, a most solemn thought.   She never
for a moment questioned her lover's affection; she
never for a moment doubted his great, warm, noble
heart; she never for a moment doubted her own love;
she knew he was more precious to her than life itself,
but she dreaded the taking of those vows which were
to change her abode, her name, her friends, and to sever
all the ties of youth.   ·At this moment she remembered the words of the marriage ceremony as performed in her own church, she remembered that she
must promise to render service and obedience for the
comfort he was to bestow upon her, and she did not
shrink from the promises which she was expected to
make, nor did she repine, nor think it unfair that so
much more was exacted of wives than of husbands.

Mr. Dana observed these evidences of thought on
her brow; he imagined a cloud had passed over her
heart—he attributed it to the right cause, and his esteem, his admiration for his chosen companion were—
if such could be—augmented.   With renewed vows
of love, of tenderness, he declared he would be always true to her, that he would always cherish her,
that he would always protect her.

Oh man! why dost thou promise what thou mayst not be able to perform?

Canst thou or woman either bind thy affections to an object which perchance may deceive thee? if from an angel of light, it turn to an angel of darkness; if it evidence to thee every day of its life, qualities, deceitful, disgusting, hateful, thou must either fall, thou must be dragged downward with it in its degradation, or thou must revolt, soul and heart from thy allegiance. Make, therefore, no rash promises, the present alone is thine—thou canst not answer for thy future.

Mr. Dana departed, and Mr. Lincoln's manner (Mary could not fail to perceive) was very troubled, but while she sympathized with him, she attributed his unhappiness to her mother's sickness. Mrs. Lincoln had been quite ill of a fever, but as she was now slowly convalescent, Mary saw no reason that her father should be unnecessarily troubled. She scarcely knew how to mention her approaching marriage to him, but she felt this was an unpleasant duty which must soon be undertaken. She had very little time in which to make her last preparations; it is true there was not much to do, for Mr. Dana had especially desired a small wedding, which request accorded entirely with her own views, and she felt sure would be agreeable to her father, in this rather delicate state of his wife's health; but Mary felt it was time to break the news to Gertrude. All day she had been trying to make up her mind to consult her father in the evening, and with this trial staring her in the face, she was full of dread at the tea-table, although she made a desperate

effort to seem unconcerned, even cheerful. But Mr.
Lincoln anticipated the interview, and invited his
daughter to a conference in the parlor, immediately
after the evening meal. Mary trembled as she seated
herself beside her father, scarcely knowing what he
would say, but expecting it was on the subject which
now occupied every thought. Imagine her surprise
as her father commenced :

"Mary, I am indeed most wretched, most miserable ; the idea that you will *ever* be the wife of this
Dana, is more than I can bear. I have been told lately,
by a person who is familiar with his whole life, who
has known his associations, his whole history, his
business affairs, his character, that he is not what he
seems. He is dissipated, he is poor, he is utterly
unable to take care of you, he is incapable of making
you happy, he has grossly deceived you. My first
fears were correct; he is nothing but an adventurer.
My child, I can never, *never* consent to this union.
The proofs I have of his bad living are indisputable ;
he is not the man you think him, depend upon it. Oh!
save yourself now, quickly—while there is yet time—
before the words are spoken which will consign you
to a life-long misery !"

. Mary said not a word; a thousand emotions filled
her ; surprise, grief, terror, wretchedness, pride, distrust, and she sat with burning cheeks and throbbing
pulse, her head bowed down.

When her father first spoke, she revolted at the
idea, her whole nature denied the hypocrisy of the
man she believed supremely noble, supremely truth-

ful. She felt she could not be deceived in his character, she had loved him so long, and so well; his letters so full, so frank, even so pious, attested his good-living, proved to her young heart his sincerity, his honor, that he was all she could ask; but when Mr. Lincoln told her of his *well-known* dissipation, indignation that he should so have blinded her, was the ruling emotion. And when her father said the second time, "I can never consent, Mary," she replied, while a proud look of defiance flashed from her eyes, "And neither will *I* consent to be the bride of a man who has so deceived me."

She rose and went slowly to her room, while Mr. Lincoln sought the presence of his invalid wife.

In her chamber, what thoughts, what griefs filled her soul! In the gloom of the evening, there like a statue she sat, nor stirred nor moved, except the throbbing heart, as she gathered up courage to look at her crumbling happiness—her faded hopes—her charmed anticipations, all vanished! as she looked into the dark, blank future, lighted by no love, cheered by no affection, bereft of him on whose bosom, yesterday, she vowed eternal, never-ending vows of constancy, of adoration!—and where was *he* now? journeying on, thinking of her? picturing bright days, when she would be all in all to him? She was indeed all in all to him now—light, pride, joy, love—all, all that heart could wish, or hope attain!

Not long did Mary Lincoln sit gloomy, mournful, wretched, and alone. She heard approaching footsteps, and rose to light the gas. With trembling hand she silently placed a chair for her father, who entered her room. He said (for Mr. Lincoln was a business man):

"Mary, you must write immediately to Mr. Dana; you must write requesting that this engagement between you be broken. See! here are paper, pen and ink;" and Mr. Lincoln opened his daughter's portfolio and placed the writing materials on the little table before her.

"And what shall I say, father?" she asked in a voice and manner fearfully cold.

"Tell him that well-proven stories have come to your ears, of his unworthiness to be the husband of any woman—much less of Mary Lincoln. Tell him as gently as you please, my daughter—as tenderly as you can—do not wound his feelings more than possible, although, rest assured, he deserves a bitter chastisement. Tell him as gently as you can—soften your language—desiring merely that you may be released—that the engagement may be broken," said Mr. Lincoln.

Mary took the pen from her father's hand—she bent over the paper—she wrote calmly, collectedly the words which were to separate her forever from one in whom her whole heart, within the last year, had been centered—one who had filled her waking thoughts—one who had wandered with her in her dreams—one who was, indeed, never absent from her vision—one whose love had so brightened her young life, who had changed her from the pensive, dreary child, to the bright, the hopeful woman. As she saw that love, his love, receding—as she felt that, hence-forth, he must be nothing to her, and she must be nothing to him—as she knew that, henceforth, her life would be desolation, and what would be his—lonely, miserable, uncared for!—she laid her head on the table before her, and burst into such an agony of sobs as seemed almost to rend her being.

Her father, surprised and alarmed, walked uneasily her chamber floor—he bent over her, and tried to soothe, to calm her; but his efforts were all vain. How cold his kisses, compared with those which would never more be hers—his voice, with that which should never more address her! Her wretchedness seemed to overwhelm her. Signed and sealed, the fatal let-ter which robbed her of years of happiness, carried disappointment and desolation to her friend!

With sighs and tears she drew from her finger the ring Mr. Dana had given her, and placed it, with his package of letters, in the hand of her father.

Mary did not once shut her eyes through the long, weary night. A burning fever coursed through her veins, and in the morning, when she changed the afternoon dress she had worn the evening before, for her usual morning attire, and laved her face, prepara-tory to a visit to her mother's chamber, she was startled to see, in the glass, her scarlet color and swelled eyelids.

When she entered Mrs. Lincoln's room, and after she had inquired about her health, and how she had rested during the night, Mrs. Lincoln suddenly said:

"Well, Mary! I suppose, you feel very unhappy, this morning?"

Mary did not reply.

Mrs. Lincoln continued:

"Your father tells me, he has lately received accounts of William Dana, that are not at all satisfactory. He has bad habits, and has been *very unfortunate in business*. My advice to you, and to every woman, is, *never* marry a *poor* man, as you value your comfort and your happiness—*never* marry a poor man, I tell you! This love in a cottage ignores servants; presupposes red hands, red face, bent-up figure—bent with hard work—a cross, fretful disposition, impaired health, a life from which all ease, all comfort, all pleasure, all elegant leisure is banished. How can a woman expect to retain the affection of her husband—how can she be charming to him—how can she be fascinating to others, when she is weighed down with cares, anxieties, and hard labor? How can she expect to be agreeable, to be 'seduisante,' when she must wear the everlasting apron of Mrs. Joe Gargery—the apron full of complaints, of reproaches, of regrets—when the eternal burden of her mournful cry is, 'Ah, mon Dieu, comme je suis fatiguée?' Take my advice, Mary, *never* marry a poor man."

Mary was confounded at these words of Mrs. Lincoln. Her heart revolted at the sentiments they expressed; where was pity, where was sympathy? she had expected that some tenderness would have been elicited, at least, for the man in whose cause her mother had before assiduously labored.

This worldliness, this cold-heartedness, this absence of all nobility of feeling; this littleness, this detestable meanness, in Mary's eyes, filled her with distrust, with condemnation of her mother; and from henceforth her esteem for her father's wife sank many, many degrees, and her attachment to the friend who had been so short a time before honored, praised by these same lips that had now turned against him, revived in all its force. The regrets that now stirred her—her self-reproaches, her fear that she was rendering him miserable, so acted upon her, as to throw her into a violent fever. For days she lingered between life and death. The struggle was desperate. Mr. Lincoln scarcely ever quitted his daughter's room. Night and day he bent over her with the soothing potion, with the cooling application; he smoothed her pillow, he moistened her parched lips, he stroked gently back the great masses of waving hair that fell across her forehead. His smothered grief and his despair were consuming him, and with it all, indignation against the woman who bore his name, and whose victim he could not but think now lay before him. — Who now, Mrs. Lincoln, came between you and his love?

Celebrated physicians were called in; but all their skill seemed of no avail—the fever was not quelled, consciousness was not restored.

To a distance Mr. Lincoln sent for men of reputation—one of them came. He stood by the bedside, and the father, anxiously regarding his dying child, said with a quivering lip, hanging for life on the physician's answer :

" Doctor, is there hope ? " and the doctor gravely shook his head, and solemnly said :

"I can give you no encouragement, sir ;" while returning life and returning reason came slowly to the young patient lying helplessly before them.

Who she was! where she was! in what state! began dimly to be realized in her extreme weakness. A dawning sense of her approaching departure crept over her ; and as she understood the doctor's words, a glad peace took possession of her—no fear of death disturbed, no dread alarmed her.

"When the gates of heaven are reached, Oh, my soul!" she thought, " and thou art safe from sin, from misery, from wretchedness, there wilt thou find joy and gladness in the light and the glory of the loved Redeemer—there, where all tears are wiped away."

The doctor quietly went out, and Mr. Lincoln, whose hope of her recovery had all died away, overcome by the realization of his worst fears, overcome by sorrow, fell on his knees by the bedside. On the cold hand of Mary his burning tears dropped, and alone in that chamber of death, that strong man sobbed like a child : " Oh, my daughter! my daughter! I have done this, I alone am responsible. I would have saved thee from sorrow more ͵bitter than the grave; and see, I have lost thee forever—lost thee with all my wealth of love unknown to thee, untold, unsuspected. Oh God! how wrong it was to hide from her all through her young life my pride of her, my affection, my sympathizing word, in her last distress. And now I lose her forever, and I am desolate, with all my sins upon my head."

Oh! then how Mary Lincoln *tried* to say " my father!" but the words died on her pale lips.

CHAPTER XXII.

MARY rose from her sick bed, feeble, but very calm, and very heavenly. She seemed to bear no ill will to any one; she strove to forget the past; she strove to smile, to be cheerful, but it was very difficult. Friends flocked round her, and congratulated her upon her recovery, and wondered why so healthy a person should have been so suddenly stricken down. Slowly came returning health—who knows whether it would ever have been wooed back had not Mary so unexpectedly heard her father's words of lament and self-reproach! When she sat alone, the consciousness of his affection, solaced her for past sorrow and soothed her present regret. It is true, there were times when her spirits were very weak, when, spite of herself, she felt that from henceforth she had no aim in life, no ambition, no hope. She strove to overcome her selfishness, so she deemed this feeling, and to rise superior to circumstances.

"Let it be my duty now," she said, "to soothe those who mourn, to bind up the broken hearted, to lighten the burden of the heavy laden. Surely," she said, with a sweet, sad smile, "my experience will not render me unfit for such a service."

Toward Mrs. Lincoln, whose health was uncertain, she bore herself kindly. She was even devoted to her, attentive to all her little wants, for she thought, if I love those only who love me, how much better am I than those who do not experience the sentiments of the Christian?

In December, Caroline Thomas was married, and Mr. Laralde accompanied Mary to the wedding, to which assembly Mary went, still pale and feeble, but urged by her father, who was most tenderly careful of her, and so solicitous for her happiness, that Mary could not but be sensible of this great change toward her.

Mary congratulated her friend upon her happy prospects, and endeavored to sympathize warmly with her.

A short time afterward, Gertrude came to spend the night with Mary in her new room, where she had been removed during her sickness.

Mrs. Lincoln did not approve of the change, but Mr. Lincoln insisted, and even went out himself, and bought several elegant articles to render it more agreeable and more beautiful to his daughter. She should never be turned out of this room, he said, never—as long as she lived. He also settled upon her a handsome income, so that she felt herself now quite raised above petty cares, and was doubly grateful to the kind author of her comfort.

Gertrude and Mary spoke of Caroline Thomas'

wedding, which was discussed freely in all circles
and whose magnificence had never been surpassed,
in their city.   Mary mentioned Mr. Laralde, and in-
cidentally she said:

"Oh! Gertrude, as he came home with me after the
wedding, he talked of you, and said, 'I do hope Miss
Gertrude does not imagine I am in love with her.'
I was very indignant, Gertrude," she continued, "for
Mr. Laralde has been so devoted to you—so much so,
I am sure, as to make us believe he was deeply at-
tached to you."

Gertrude did not reply; indeed she spoke no more
that night, and Mary soon fell asleep.

What was her surprise the next morning when she
woke very early, to see Gertrude walking the floor,
clasping her hands in seeming distress, while tears
rolled down her cheeks.

"Oh, dear Gertrude," said Mary, as she sprang to
her friend and threw her arms around her, "are you
sick?   Do tell me what is the matter?"

Gertrude, ashamed and surprised, endeavored to
hide her tears, but it was too late.

"I am not sick, dear Mary," she replied, "except
with regret that you should have witnessed this weakness.   I have not slept, your words caused me such
pain here," she said, laying her hand on her heart,
"that I do not believe I shall ever sleep again.   I
loved him, Mary Lincoln! I loved him more than I
can tell!   I hung on his words!   I listened breathlessly to their music.   I dwelt for hours on his flat-
tery.   I hugged his honied phrases to my heart—and

he deliberately deceived me! He trifled with me for his amusement—hypocrite that he is! But it is all well, thus am I punished for my disloyalty to my noble father! and as I see this sweet dream take its flight, I vow, never to place myself in so humiliating a position again. Oh, Mary! Mary!" she went on, " you never can know the suffering those words of his give me, for you are too strong, too brave, to love so unwisely."

Mary would have told Gertrude that she was able to sympathize with her, from experience, but she did not wish to exhume buried grief.

The next day, Kate Lee came blushingly to tell Mary that she was soon to be married to Mr. Laralde, and to beg her to officiate as bridemaid at the ceremony. Mary declined on the plea of health not fully established, but she did not communicate the news to Gertrude, thinking it wiser that she should hear it from another source, and hoping that ere that time her sorrows would be softened.

A year passed away without many changes to Mary Lincoln. She made several short trips during this time, once with Mr. Clifford and Gertrude; once with Mr. and Mrs. Day and Gertrude. These journeys were usually pleasant. Mary's enthusiasm seemed to have died away, but her friends gave her credit for more quiet enjoyment, perhaps, than she experienced. At times, the waves of sorrow and regret would, spite of her efforts, roll over her soul; old memories often caused her poignant suffering. She strove to banish the past; she prayed most fervently to God for help, but after all she was but a poor, weak, sorrowing human being. Oh! those regrets! Oh! those remembrances, what mournful tears they yet caused her!

One evening, as Mrs. Lincoln and Mary were seated in the parlor, Mr. Lincoln came in, and handed to his wife a letter postmarked New York, and sealed with black. Mrs. Lincoln opened the note which was written in an unknown hand. Could Mary have seen it, she would immediately have recognized the penmanship, as that of the sister-in-law of Mr. Dana.

Mrs. Lincoln read, and thoughtlessly exclaimed, "Poor Dana! died two weeks ago."

(Mary swooned, but Mrs. Lincoln did not heed.)

"And, oh, Mary! he died with your blest name on his lips."

CHAPTER XXIII.

Two years again, and Mary now, in the full perfection of youth, subdued by sorrow, made stronger and gentler by suffering, felt the anguish of disappointed hope and love gradually subsiding, and could look with calmness on the storms of her earlier life; a guardian angel to her father, respected and admired by her mother, to whom she found herself necessary, a beloved and honored friend, a true, sincere Christian, the world began again to put on its charms for her, and to smile again upon her in its beauty.

This autumn, Mr. and Mrs. Lincoln were going on a long journey, and intended to take Bessie with them. As Susan wished to go to her friends, and Mary did not care to travel, she thought it would now be a good opportunity to pay Gertrude a long contemplated visit. The house was accordingly closed, and Mary was delightfully installed at Mr. Clifford's. The neighborhood around Mr. Clifford's was still slowly increasing, but the charm of all were Gertrude and the kind and elegant Mrs. Day.

O! what a "glory did this world put on" in those gorgeous September and October days.

17

How sweet the perfume of the autumn air, laden with smells of ripe fruit—of peaches, with the soft bloom on their cheeks—of apples of every variety—of yellow quinces—of luscious. grapes, bending in all their grace and beauty from heavily laden arbors, and in bountiful vineyards; how rich the tints of fall flowers, of the gay dahlia, crimson, white, purple, yellow and streaked with varied colors! and later the asters and crysanthemums giving life and vigor to the garden scene. The queen of flowers again put forth her beauty and bloomed more exquisitely, more perfectly, than in the warm summer days. Tube roses and heliotrope gave their fragrance to the evening air. The leaves of trees and of shrubs fairly glistened in the noon-day sun, and as the days grew shorter and cooler, and the foliage ripened, Mary loved to stand at the window and gaze upon the changing tinges of the forest, their flaming crimson turning to russet, their variety of hue, their variety of shape, their different genera and species. The grass, how green in its velvet-like softness! the sky, how lovingly it seemed to bend over all created things! the air, how fresh, how invigorating, how exhilarating to the spirits and the frame!

Mary took especial delight in the mowing of the fields. The laborers busily at work, piling immense stacks of yellow new-made hay, and gathering it in great wagons, preparatory to storing it away for winter, was a scene which contrasted so greatly with the quiet of the landscape that she looked on with intense enjoyment.

What charming walks she took with Gertrude! what agreeable, refined, warm-hearted people she met! what social evenings she passed, where all seemed to emulate each other in mutual affection, attention and appreciation! That neighborhood, Mary found, was indeed as Gertrude laughingly remarked: " A mutual admiration society."

But Mary's visit was drawing to a close—a week more and it would be over; why did she look forward as she never had done before, with a tender regret to parting from her friends. Did she believe in presentiments? Did she feel it was her last stay under that hospitable roof; was it that her love for those who had always been so kind to her was strengthening and growing with accumulating years? There are some who believe that as age creeps on, our capacity for loving enlarges, increases and intensifies.

At the end of October, during one afternoon, which Mary never ceased to remember, Gertrude and herself quitted the house to take a walk, and to pay a visit to a neighbor, Mrs. Allan.

As they passed the lodge at the gate, and reached the main road, Gertrude said, " What a delicious evening! how glorious it is !"

Mary responded heartily, for she felt in every pulse of her being, the truth of her companion's observation.

It was indeed a magnificent evening!

" I do not need, dear Gertrude," said Mary, " the soul of Walt Vander Harnish to appreciate and enjoy the scene outspread before us, but I would give much for the pencil of Jean Paul to portray it, and emotions to which it gives rise."

"No, dear Mary," said Gertrude, "we who know you intimately, are aware that you need borrow no inspiration from others, your own soul is full of poetry."

What a difference in people! have you never observed it! How many, who consider themselves criterions of taste, of elegance, indeed as models in all things, would be very much startled were any one to insinuate to them, that what they imagined they possessed was all a dream, but who nevertheless resemble in one respect, at least, Peter Bell.

> " A primrose by the river's brink,
> A yellow primrose was to him,
> And it was nothing more.
>
> The soft blue sky did never melt
> Into his heart,—he never felt
> The witchery of the soft blue sky."

"Do you never recall those words of the lamented Mrs. Jameson: 'With what different eyes may people view the same things!' 'We receive but what we give,' says the poet, and all the light and glory and beauty with which certain things are in a manner *suffused* to the eye of fancy, must issue from our own souls, and be reflected back to us, else 't is all in vain.

> ' We may not hope from outward things to win
> The passion and the life whose fountains are within.' "

"The sentiment is as true as she has beautifully

expressed it, and I have often remembered it," replied Mary.

Subsiding into silence now, each regarding the sky and the smiling landscape, they wended their way over the smooth road, while a cheerful stillness reigned around, unbroken save by the tinkling of bells, and the sweet song of happy birds late returning to their nests. How charming was nature in this lovely hour! how rich the hues of evening! In the patches of forest all round them, the trees were nearly all quite leaf-less, and the great trunks reared up their giant pro-portions, and traced their delicate stems upon the golden sky. At a distance the towers of the village church loomed up, every turret glittering in the set-ting sun.

"We miss the sweet-scented hay-cocks, the trees laden with fruit, the richly dyed leaves of the earlier autumn," said Mary, breaking silence, and speaking almost as if to herself, "but instead of those we have this delicious air, which sends new life and renewed activity to both mind and body."

"Yes," said Gertrude, "it is all charming; these country walks are delightful, even when I am all alone. Dear mother Nature, is the queen I worship; how I love to muse upon her wonders! to talk to her and listen to her teachings; for every day and every hour another lesson she gives us, for she is always new and always young. How she speaks to us, on the hill and in the valley; in sylvan shades or under a single tree, in the green bursting leaf after cheerless days; in the bud which unfolds beneath gentle showers, and the

warm sunlight; in the small beginnings of spring, and
the great terminations of autumn; in the little brook
gliding off ripplingly at our feet, mayhap to meet the
great ocean; in the small pebble, the tiny insect, the
noisome weed which springs up to surround, and cut
off, and crush out our tender plants. She teaches us
perseverance and patience, which cause us to rejoice
in the fruition of our labors. And then the rains, and
the snows, and the cold frosts and ice of winter, when
the beauty and the joy of the year are crisped and
withered, and swallowed up—as it were in gloom—do
they not remind us of similar scenes in our lives?"
and her voice dropped to a sad tone; " when darkness
and clouds hung over us, and we almost shrank from
the trials, the austerities of life. But, thank God!
after darkness comes light, after winter comes spring,
and the sun once again rises cloudless, and the soft
airs of happiness cause roses to spring up and blossom in our hearts. I have often thought," she continued, " the joy which comes after sorrow, is more intense the longer it is withheld, and I am often reminded,
dear Mary, of those words of your former scrap-book :
'Adversity is like the period of the latter rain, cold,
comfortless, unfriendly to man and to animals, yet
from that season have their birth, the flower, the fruit
and the pomegranate.   And again :

'What tho' o'er the long spring, snow drifts cold were booming,
The leaf rises greener from sheltering snow.' "

Gertrude now stopped before the house of Mrs. Allan, and as she slowly unfastened the gate, she smiled

and said : "Do not think I am melancholy, dear friend, I have had so little real sorrow in my life that I scarcely feel as if I knew what it meant; though in former times I did consider myself a victim. My troubles, however, were imaginary, and I have since often laughed over them, and congratulated myself that they were only blessings in disguise."

"There are a great many imaginary, as well as real, troubles," said Mary, "and I doubt not but the imaginary ones cause quite as much unrest, quite as much suffering as the real ones."

"I suppose," said Gertrude, " that those who come to the close of a long life, and look back upon each action, find that events realized, according to their desires, would have caused far greater misery than their early disappointments."

Mary thought of her own dead hopes—the thought, however, did not banish pain for the past, nor diminish the affection, the respect for the memory of him who was laid at rest. She still remembered him, as he had been to her, and still at times, alas! deeply regretted him.

Mrs. Allan was at home, and in her cosy parlor. The piano stood open, and books and work were scattered over the large table. Beautiful vines clambered over the picture frames, and vases and baskets of crimson leaves and green berries, cheered the pretty room. When they entered, Mrs. Allan's venerable mother, Mrs. Warner, sat at a table drawing. Mary was very much amazed that a lady who numbered eighty years should draw so finely, so very delicately, and expressed her surprise to that effect.

"My eyes arc yet very strong, my dear Miss Lincoln, and sketching is so great a pleasure, and I have so many lovely pictures, and so many delightful views in this beautiful country spot, that I could indulge myself all day long in this occupation and not be weary; and I am often so carried away in the enjoyment of this recreation, that night comes before I am aware of it."

"Then you like the country, Mrs. Warner?" asked Mary.

"It is my darling theme," replied Mrs. Warner.

"I have heard, said Mary, turning to Mrs. Allan, "that Mrs. Allan was formerly very much opposed to country life."

"Yes," said Mrs. Allan with a merry laugh, "Mr. Allan, for years, tried to persuade me to live in the country, but I imagined such a life equal to that of a banished convict, or to being buried alive, and I would not consent on any condition. He offered me, year after year, almost baronial residences, all of which I firmly declined, preferring even a small house, in town, to a large one in the country; but finally, one day, taking an unaccountable woman's freak, or perhaps being brought over by his persuasions, I said I was willing, provided a pretty place could be found. Mr. Allan speedily set himself to work to procure a suitable home, and in a short time, luckily, we heard of this spot, which we liked, and immediately purchased."

"Were you happy the first year?" asked Mary.

"The first two years, I absolutely *dreamed* away,"

answered Mrs. Allan. "Every morning I went into the garden, gathered my flowers, brought them into my little library, and arranged them as tastefully as possible, placed my Æolian harp in the window, dressed myself for the day, drew up my great easy chair and my stool, took an interesting book and seated myself at the table. Here, seldom disturbed by any one, breathing the perfume of my bouquet, I read or wrote, and mused sometimes during an entire day, and my only regret was, that my former life had been wasted in so frivolous a manner. At length, I suddenly woke to find I had worn out everything I had. I remember I very much shocked my nearest neighbor, almost a stranger to me, by asking her, one day, when she called, if she could lend me a night-dress. She opened her eyes very wide, I can assure you, but when I repeated my question, and told her I had examined cedar chests and closets in vain, in my search for something to wear, she laughed heartily, and advised me to go to work and forswear dream-life, in future. Since that time my children have returned from school, and my dear mother has taken up her abode with me; so that I have given up reveries, and sentiment, and school-girl fancies, particularly as the custom does not suit well with my years."

Mary smiled, and thought Mrs. Allan's first experience of country life pleasing, a little novel, indeed, quite a contrast to the usual mode.

The friends now rose to go, as the twilight was short, and they had only time to get home before dark.

When they were once more on the road, retracing their steps, Mary said:

"Did you ever see so lovely, so beautiful, so interesting an old lady as Mrs. Warner? She is certainly very picturesque, with her silver hair, her clear, exquisite complexion, her snow-white cap, and, above all, her motherly, gentle, lady-like manners. What a character she would make for some romance-writer!"

"Yes," replied Gertrude, "she is very accomplished, and, with her experience of life, her wisdom, her knowledge, her fine conversational powers, she is really captivating. What a lesson may we all learn, from her example, to go on every day unfolding, and, like the celebrated Cosmo de Medici, never be too old to learn!"

Just at that moment they saw two persons on horseback, coming toward them—a lady and gentleman. They soon discovered the lady to be no other than Mrs. Day, on her white horse Earl Grey, and the tall, dark-haired, distinguished-looking gentleman was a stranger to Mary—who was he?

Mrs. Day and her companion stopped, and while Mrs. Day's superb horse pawed the ground, and arched his graceful neck, his mistress said with a smile:

"Mr. Etheridge, Miss Clifford, your former friend; Mr. Etheridge, Miss Lincoln."

"Oh!" said Gertrude, "when did you come, Mr. Etheridge? I did not even know that you were expected. I am *very* glad to see you!"

Mr. Etheridge bowed to both young ladies, and in

reply to Gertrude, said he had arrived that very day from Philadelphia, where he had spent the last month.

"Do not forget, young ladies," said Mrs. Day, "your promise to come this evening and see the new picture. It was hung this morning, and Mr. Day is in a fever of anxiety to hear Mr. Clifford's criticisms upon it. Tell Mr. Clifford, for me, that I expect him very early."

Saying adieu, she touched her horse lightly with her whip, and bounded away, and Mr. Etheridge raised his black silk cap to the ladies and rode away, closely following his companion.

"How graceful and easy she is on horseback," said Mary. "I had no idea she rode so well!"

"She rides elegantly," replied Gertrude. "Mrs. Day did not tell me she was looking for Mr. Etheridge."

"Who is Mr. Etheridge?" asked Mary. "I have never heard of him before."

"It is strange you have not met him here; he has made several visits to Mrs. Day, who is a relative of his, but he usually remains a very short time. He lives in New Orleans, but spends his summers at the East."

The name of that city smote Mary—it always did.

"He is a very splendid gentleman," Gertrude went on; "I can testify to his manners and graces. Mrs. Day thinks he is as perfect as humanity can be. I wish to warn you now of her lavish praises of him, for he is a confirmed bachelor, Miss Mary Lincoln, and it is useless to fall in love with him."

"Oh, there is no danger! I am not at all susceptible, even were Mr. Etheridge ten times more attractive than you would lead me to imagine," said Mary,
laughing, while a sigh involuntarily escaped her.

"I believe you, Mary," said Gertrude, "I never
heard of your liking, or being *partial* even, to any
gentleman."

"No!" said Mary, while a flush overspread her
features, which, happily, Gertrude did not see.

CHAPTER XXIV.

As Mr. Clifford closed the hall-door, after tea, Mary walked to the marble balustrade, and looked up at the full moon. The air was cool, and she drew her thin shawl tightly round her graceful figure.

"What a magnificent night, Gertrude," said she; "do you think this can be our Indian summer?"

"Oh, no!" Mr. Clifford replied; "our hazy days have not yet come; we must first have a little winter-time, you know; we have not had any frost yet, or at least, so little of it as to be scarcely perceptible."

"But, papa," said Gertrude, "the trees are nearly leafless."

"Yes, my daughter," answered Mr. Clifford, "but this year it is their natural decay which has stripped them from the stem; have you not observed their gradual ripening?"

"No, papa," she responded.

"How delightful the autumn has been, this year! I never experienced so beautiful an October before; perhaps the happiness of being with friends has had much to do with my enjoyment of nature at this season. I am sure, I never shall forget all this pleasure, and I never shall be able to return your kindness," said Mary, with a shade of timidity in her voice.

" Our pleasure, in your society, has been quite as great as any you have received, Miss Mary," said Mr. Clifford, " and our only regret is, that your visit can not be prolonged."

" Nothing would be more agreeable than to remain; believe me, these are very happy hours spent under your roof, Mr. Clifford ; but I am needed at home. I am so enamored of country, or rather, suburban life, that I should like to persuade my father to adopt it as his own ; but *mother*, I know, would never consent," said Mary.

" It would be charming ! " exclaimed Gertrude, " to have you on the place adjoining. It is for sale, is it not, papa ? "

" Yes, my love," replied Mr. Clifford, " and I think the Mowbray place one of the most desirable spots in the country. The grounds are quite extensive, the house is modern, commodious, well-built, and really handsome. The orchards are of the choicest fruits ; in short, it comprises every comfort, and every desirable convenience."

" Oh, how happy I should be," said Mary, " if father could be induced to buy it. I think he has a secret longing for the country; indeed, I have often heard him express his desire to that effect; I am sure he awaits only a word from mother, who, as I said before, does not give him much encouragement."

" Do try and persuade Mrs. Lincoln," said Gertrude ;

"we should like to have her always near us—to say nothing of Mr. and Miss Lincoln."

"When I return home I will use every argument I have," said Mary, laughing, "but without much hope, I fear."

Thus talking, the friends pursued their way, taking the short road to Mr. Day's.

Mr. and Mrs. Day and Mr. Etheridge were in the drawing-room as they entered. Mr. Etheridge was very warmly greeted by Mr. and Miss Clifford and was again presented to Mary.

Something in his dark, magnificent, soul-lit eyes, sent a sunshine to Mary's heart. The ease, and grace and elegance of his movement and manner, combined with the clear, low tones of his silvery voice, and the dignity of his bearing, caused an involuntary feeling of respect and admiration. With a slight trembling she took the seat beside him which chance offered her, and listened with strange sensation to the thoughts, from time to time, he eloquently worded.

But Mr. Clifford soon, in a lull of friendly commérage, said, "Mrs. Day, I am all impatience to see the new picture; I fear I can wait no longer, will you permit me to look at it?"

"Certainly, Mr. Clifford," replied the mistress of the house, as she rose, and all in the room rose at the same time, and Mr. Day adjusted the lights to good advantage.

"We are very anxious to hear how you like it."

The group placed themselves in good positions, instantly aware of the great beauty of the production.

But Mr. Clifford was not long silent; soon from his lips burst, "Oh, c'est beau! c'est magnifique! c'est charmant! c'est ravissant! c'est ravissant!"

Mary stood with her friends before the heavenly creation; it was a saint, "Saint Agnes," and as she looked at the exquisite beauty of figure, of feature, of light and shade, of expression, she was selfish enough to wish that Mr. Clifford would not be so demonstrative in his manifestations of delight. His words of admiration grated on her ear. She felt that it was almost sacrilege to *speak* in the presence of that divine beauty, how much more then to criticise the well-shaped arm, the hands, the up-turned melting eyes: she almost wished she was alone with it, that she might comprehend its "emotional soul." Was it penitence for past sin that unsealed the fountain of those tears? or was it spoken pardon that shone in that ecstatic face? or was it hope, and love, and faith in her Redeemer that beamed in the soft radiance of those meek eyes?

While Mary stood rapt in the holy thoughts which glowed on her sweet cheek, gradually the circle around her stole away to their seats—all but one, who also lost to time and place, stood rapt in the living, breathing picture at his side.

Mary started at last from her pure dream, and suddenly looked up to meet the eyes of her companion bent on her, with so much interest, with so much sympathy as sent a thrill through her, such as she had not known for three long weary years.

"I hope I have not interrupted your contemplation,

Miss Lincoln?" said Mr. Etheridge, "Oh, no," said Mary, smiling consciously, as she felt that Mr. Etheridge had divined her thoughts. It was strange! at that moment the words of Gertrude passed through her mind, "do not fall in love with him, for it is useless, my dear."

A blush that she should for a second have entertained such a thought, deepened on cheek, and brow, and neck, and she turned to seek her former place at the fireside.

"How do you like the picture, Miss Mary," asked Mr. Day, as he rose and placed a chair for her.

"Oh, I can not tell, it has a wonderful power over me—it makes me dizzy, overwhelms me. I have been in Rome since I last spoke to you, Mr. Day," she said, with a melancholy smile and a sigh. "I saw the Forum, the little band of Christians, the demons, mad accusers of this youth, this grace and piety, and then this superb head, bent to the executioner." She stopped and reddened, as if she had said too much.

"The picture impresses me, too, somewhat sadly," said Mrs. Day.

Mr. Day left the room, as if in search of something, and returned with several photographs—Raphael's Madonnas; some of Coreggio, of Leonardo da Vinci, of Pietro Perugino, of Andrea del Sarto, and copies of other famous pictures.

With deep interest Mary regarded these photographs, which those who had seen the originals, declared admirable.

Mrs. Day remarked that the Madonnas of Raphael
18

always stirred her with a deep inexplicable sensation, they always inspired an elevated sentiment; she always felt for hours after looking at them, as if she had been in the company of angels. Gertrude preferred the Madonna di Foligno, the Madonna del Pesce, and La Perle, to the Madonna della Seggiola and the San Sisto; she thought, in the San Sisto, the countenance of the Virgin did not sufficiently declare the maturity of the woman, or the tenderness of the mother. In her imagination, no other emotion than surprise or youthful wonder was depicted in the face.

Mr. Etheridge politely begged leave to differ with Miss Clifford, and said he thought the San Sisto decidedly the greatest picture he had yet seen. The benign pity in this virgin's face, was to him inexpressibly touching, and in the countenance of the infant Jesus, he read His whole future life on earth.

"How the beauty and the charm of a fine picture increase, as we become more familiar with it," said Mr. Clifford.

"Yes," replied Mr. Day, "is it not so with everything of a high order, in literature, as well as in art? The poet's truly admirable production, as well as the artist's, grows upon acquaintance, at least I find it so in my case."

"It is a true observation," replied Mr. Etheridge.

When Mr. Clifford, and the young ladies said adieu, Mr. Etheridge remarked that if Miss Lincoln would permit him, he would be glad to accompany her home, the night was so fine.

Mary thanked him politely, referred him to Mr.

Clifford who had attended her, and accepted his society with pleasure.

The night was indeed lovely, the moon was at its full, and its silver sheen lighted earth and heaven. The tall shadows of the almost leafless oaks lay on the velvet lawn, and across the broad white shell road. Far from the house, paths diverged from the great avenue down through the green dell, and off up to the distant hillock, where sat a rustic bower crowned with its wealth of glistening leaves. Mary and Mr. Etheridge stopped to admire a belt of superb pines and larches, and cypresses, and the willow, whose pendent stems floated in the night air.

"How beautiful is this spot," said Mary, "I am always compelled to stay my steps here and admire it. Those cypresses, whose leaves are now quite yellow, are magnificent specimens."

"Yes," replied Mr. Etheridge, "it is truly a fit dwelling-place for Oberon and Titania."

The great iron gate was open, and as Mary and her escort stepped out to the main road, they found that Mr. Clifford and Gertrude, who were just in advance, had taken the long way home.

Mr. Etheridge, whose thoughts went back to the Saint Agnes, asked Mary what she really thought of the new picture.

"I am no judge of art, Mr. Etheridge," she said, "I do not understand its rules at all. I know only what pleases me, but I do think that face is the most exquisitely beautiful I ever saw. Those divine upturned eyes haunt me. There is a world of expression in the hands and their attitude; the drapery strikes me as very graceful, the tints as very life-like, and the soft lights and shadows seem very rich. It is a chef d'œuvre of some celebrated artist; is it not? do you know? I did not hear Mr. Day mention the author's name."

"Yes," said Mr. Etheridge, "it is an original by Guido. Mr. Day tells me he saw it when in Rome, and was so delighted with it that he could not be contented without it. He made a great many unsuccessful efforts while there to buy it, but finally by means of a friend, accomplished his object. And well is it worth the pains and trouble which he took to obtain it. Such graceful touches of the pencil I never saw in any other picture! the shadow of the muslin which lies over the bosom; the soft sweep in the lock of hair, and the lace mingled with it, which droop behind the ear, and fall over the beautifully rounded shoulder; even the tip of the ear has its own particular character, its own lovely expression."

"I have never before seen the photographs which Mr. Day showed us," observed Mary; "they too must be a new acquisition."

"Yes," replied Mr. Etheridge, "the same friend who purchased the Guido for Mr. Day, forwarded at the same time the specimens we looked at this evening."

"It is perhaps venturing much for one who is nothing of a connoisseur, to declare that I never in my life saw a Madonna that realized my idea," observed Mary. "I think a Madonna ought to be a type of perfect womanhood in every respect, in perfection of face, of figure, of lineament, which all, I suppose, are comparatively easy for all good artists. But the exalted character, the holiness, the soul which ought to shine in the countenance of the mother of God—where do we see them? I believe you do not agree with me, Mr. Etheridge, for I think I heard you express your admiration of the San Sisto."

" I do admire it extremely, Miss Lincoln," said Mr. Etheridge.

Arrived at the porter's lodge, Mr. Etheridge asked Mary if her visit at Mr. Clifford's would be long, and when she said she expected to return to town on the following morning, he said he had hoped to have the pleasure of calling upon Miss Clifford and herself on the morrow.

Mary replied that her father had written her a note to-day, saying he would send the carriage for her, and as both himself and her mother had been absent during a long time, it was necessary that she should return home.

Mr. Etheridge then remarked that Mr. Lincoln was an old friend of his, and that he had had business relations with him of many years standing, and that he had been very much puzzled this evening trying to imagine where Miss Lincoln was, when he had dined two years ago with Mr. and Mrs. Lincoln, at their residence.

" Were you ever at our house?" asked Mary, rather agreeably startled.

"I certainly spent several delightful hours there, at the time of which I speak," was the response.

"Are you sure it was at my father's?" asked Mary.

"Yes," replied Mr. Etheridge smiling, "and Mr. Day was with me."

"I can not imagine where I was," said Mary. "I am sure I am sorry I was not at home."

"No one regrets it so much as myself, Miss Lincoln, said Mr. Etheridge, with a grave tone, "but I will do myself the honor of calling upon Mrs. Lincoln and yourself, before I return to the south."

"Do you go soon?" inquired Mary, with a little trepidation in her tone.

"The day after to-morrow," was the answer.

Mr. Clifford and Gertrude were on the porch awaiting Mary and her companion. As the hour was late, Mr. Etheridge did not enter, but lifted his black silk cap as he said good night, and retraced his steps.

After Gertrude and Mary had retired to their chamber, Gertrude said to her friend, with a merry twinkling of the eye, "I hope, dear child, you remembered my instructions of this evening."

Mary blushed, and said, "I will not deny that I thought of them once or twice, and I thank you, Miss Clifford, for putting me on my guard. Mr. Etheridge is certainly an elegant gentleman, and I can readily perceive his society might be fatal to the peace of a *susceptible* person."

"I am of your opinion," was the reply.

Mary Lincoln could not sleep that night; visions of soft, black eyes, of a noble figure, of bright glances, floated before her; tender, low, melting tones still murmured in her ear. She accused herself of weakness, of forgetfulness of the past, of unfaithfulness to the memory of former affections. She wished she had never seen Mr. Etheridge—then, she was glad she had met him, for her heart humbly acknowledged there was one, in the wide, dreary world, of whom she could think with interest, and who, she felt, might be a friend. Then she had no hope that she should see him more than once again, for she knew he would soon take his departure for his sunny home.

On the next morning, Mary took an affectionate leave of Gertrude and her father, and thanked them heartily for their kind attentions during her long and delightful visit. Gertrude promised to return the compliment very soon, and with many an embrace, they parted.

Mr. and Mrs. Lincoln welcomed their daughter so warmly, and were so glad to be at home, although they had had an unusually agreeable journey, and it was so pleasant to be united again, that Mary felt quite happy. She had not much to relate; time in the country is, though charming and enjoyable, not easily described by city people. However she spoke of her visits, her walks with Gertrude, and she did not forget to tell her father of the place for sale, adjoining Mr. Clifford's, and to wish, with all her heart, that he would purchase it. ⋆ Mr. Lincoln smiled encouragingly, but Mrs. Lincoln said that Mary need put no such ideas into her father's head, for she would never take up her abode in the country—she might as well die at once.

Mary did not forget to speak of Mr. Etheridge.

Mr. Lincoln was glad to hear that Mr. Etheridge was at Mr. Day's, and hoped he should have the pleasure of seeing him before his departure. He took the opportunity of descanting, with high appreciation, on his excellent qualities, and the refinement and polish of his mind and manner.

Mary quietly remarked that he had mentioned his intention of coming to see them soon. She endeavored to hide from herself her feverish desire to meet him again, but at every ring of the door bell all the next day, she started in anxious expectation.

Mr. Etheridge did not come, and with great disappointment Mary Lincoln gave up hope, and tried to forget that she had ever seen him.

Three or four days passed, and in the evening, Mr. and Mrs. Lincoln and Mary sat in the cheerful sitting-room. Mary heard the door bell gently sound. It was an unfamiliar ring, and her heart beat high with returning hope.

Mr. Etheridge entered; with a firm resolve, Mary stilled the fluttering of her pulses, and joined her father and mother, in their cordial salutations to the new comer.

Mr. Etheridge was charming, was noble, was elegant, was dignified, in short was everything. Mary thought of what Gertrude had said. Other visitors entered, but he did not quit Mary's side. He talked of

Mrs. Day, of Gertrude, of his intended journey, which would take place on the morrow. He hoped to have the gratification of seeing Mr., Mrs. and Miss Lincoln in New Orleans this winter, but Mr. Lincoln said that he considered the journey so dangerous, that he dreaded it too much to make a recreation or pleasure of it. Mary's heart sunk within her, and her spirits fell many degrees as she felt that in all probability she should never meet again the only one whom earth contained, that had power to warm anew her cold heart.

Mr. Etheridge departed.

Mary's former cheerfulness was gone, and with it, also, all her former fine theories. She had felt herself strong to bear all the ills of life. She had accustomed herself, without shrinking, to stare the future in the face, to look forward to years of loneliness, perhaps of solitude, to an unloving and unloved old age—should God spare her so long. But now came a deep unrest, an inquietude, a strong, fervent prayer for love. Oh! are there not hours in every created being's experience, when we long with an intense yearning for one "half soul," when we feel that friendship is not sufficient, the heart demands and will have love.

Mary felt lowered in her own estimation, and she inwardly vowed to struggle against these infirmities, to make the life within her all soul, so that the heart might not be, or at least might not be felt, that henceforth she would look coldly on the earth.

Two days passed—Mr. Etheridge suddenly returned. He told Mr. Lincoln that he could not continue

19

on his way, but that he had been so restless, so miserable, disturbed by the fear of never meeting Mary again, or meeting her under other circumstances, that he had concluded to hasten back and dare his fate. He said he faithfully believed in the love that " at a glance, as if sun-painted, started to life at once."

With downcast eyes, Mary acknowledged a similar belief, and said, blushingly, that the first evening of her introduction to Mr. Etheridge, a look had penetrated her with new hope and new life! She told him that she did not wish to conceal the past from him, because there were some who would have the *first* affection of the object of their choice, or none— that she felt it her duty to acquaint him with her former griefs. Then Mr. Etheridge smiled sadly and said it were well to let the dead past bury its dead, and that he respected the delicacy of her sentiments, and that he trusted she would always confide in him; he said he was happy, supremely happy, and blest.

And he pressed Mr. Lincoln to allow the wedding to take place immediately. And Mr. Lincoln consented, after a little urging, for he said, if he *must* give his daughter away, he was very well satisfied to give her to such a man.

Mrs. Day and Gertrude congratulated Mr. Etheridge upon his great good luck, and complimented Mary upon the sweet qualities which had captivated their friend, and Gertrude looked mischievously and asked her why she did not obey orders, and laughingly repeated to Mr. Etheridge what she had said to Mary on the evening of his arrival.

Mr. Clifford folded Mary in his arms, first begging Mr. Etheridge's pardon, and said how sorry they would all be to part with her.

Mr. Lincoln's only objection to the match was the idea of his daughter's going so far away, but he determined that after this winter she should have a home nearer him.

The wedding was small; the bride looked lovely in her rich dress of white satin, covered with the finest lace, and her simple veil, looped back with white roses. She was very self-possessed and dignified, and graceful, and Mr. Etheridge was so happy, and so much delighted with his new wife, that admiration and love for her fairly gleamed in his face.

Gertrude rejoiced in her friend's happiness, and sighed neither for her own past, nor for her future. Bound up in her father's affection, sensible of his deprivations on her account, she had firmly resolved, never to listen to the vows she often heard, but to make him sensible that *his* love was all sufficient for her.

Mrs. Lincoln busied herself in all Mary's preparations, and shed many tears, much to Mary's surprise, at the parting.

•CHAPTER XXV.

NEARLY thirteen years had passed away since the marriage of Mary Lincoln and Mr. Etheridge. It was a June evening. The doors and windows of the stately mansion at Mowbray (the country home adjoining Clifford place), of the Etheridges, were all thrown open. The soft moonlight flooded the whole house, and the evening air, laden with the fragrance of the rose and woodbine, played in and out of the windows and dallied with the folds of the delicate lace curtains. In the large library, whose windows open to the floor of the porch on two sides of the room, were our friend Mary and her husband. The uncovered harp, the open piano, the well filled bookcases, the pamphlets and periodicals scattered here and there, the bronzes and marble statues, the choice pictures hanging on the delicately painted walls, attest the elegant tastes and pursuits of the owners and occupants.

These were all, house, grounds, furniture, adornments, purchased by Mr. Lincoln and presented to his daughter, much to her surprise and gratitude, upon her return from New Orleans, the spring after her marriage.

In a low fauteuil, in this pretty room, sat Mrs. Etheridge, while stretched at her feet, wearied with the fatigues of a day of business in town, reclined her husband, his head on her knee. Years have dealt most gently with Mary. They have not taken away with her youth its freshness, but have added to it the graces of the matron; to the expression of her features, the kind, tender, devoted love of the wife, the mother, the friend. The beaming intellect, cultivated constantly as a pleasure and a duty, shines in her soft eyes, and sparkles on her lips. No wonder her husband is as proud of her as a man can be, she who has fulfilled every desire of his heart. Constantly she has striven thus far to do her whole duty, and when the dark hours came, as they must to every one, she had struggled and prayed, and triumphed over sickness, pain and irritability. God was now, in her prosperity as well as in the sorrows of her youth, her trust, her God, and her king. He gave her strength to endure and to conquor.

An indulgent but firm mother, a true wife, gently but never failing, reproving her husband's faults of conscience, for when she married him, he was not a Christian, though a moralist; a kind, orderly mistress; an excellent manager and housekeeper ; life went on smoothly and quietly and pleasantly for all within her household. Taste and elegance reigned supreme at her table, as well as thoughout her establishment. *Her* silver was the brighest, *her* porcelaine the purest and most delicate, *her* damask the whitest and the finest, *her* viands the best cooked and the most temptingly served.

Round her husband's board, the scholar, the artist, the poet, were gathered, and there were "the feast of reason and the flow of soul."

Striving to neglect nothing, she felt how high is woman's mission, how very much it requires to be perfect; and not only did she endeavor to be the comfort of her family, but she still made efforts to keep up with the literature of the day, and not only to be her husband's housekeeper, but his best and most charming companion.

Mr. Etheridge had married her upon so short an acquaintance, and was so great a stranger to her accomplishments, that surprise, wonder, delight, seized him at the discovery of what he valued so highly.

This evening, clothed in the purest, softest white, with no ornaments except the single diamond eardrops, and the pin containing one single stone to correspond, she sat—both sat, in the moonlight.

As usual, Mr. Etheridge had discussed the news of the day—politics, art, and the latest read book. And afterward, Mary, whose motherly heart was brim full of mother's love, proceeded to relate how the day had gone with her. She had had a visit from the teacher of her eldest child—her noble ten year old boy, and her pride and hopes for him had more than ever been aroused.

"The professor says his intellect is truly splendid," observed Mrs. Etheridge.

Mr. Ethridge smiled at his wife's enthusiasm.

"It is not the *first* time, my dear, I can assure you, that different persons, entire strangers to each other, have expressed their opinion of his capacities in exactly the same words," said Mary, with pride in her tones. "You know, in music, in drawing, in history, and arithmetic; in his child's philosophy he exhibits the same powers of memory and of aptitude. And I have such good accounts of his gentlemanly behavior that I feel to-night quite thankful and encouraged. Dear little Bertha to-day brought me her A B C's, and begged mamma to teach her them, and while she repeated each one after me, evidently with the greatest enjoyment, her heavenly eyes seemed to soften with the dawning light of thought, and her curling locks tossed off her brow, she looked to me like an angel, and would have seemed so to you, too, dear, if you could have seen her."

Mr. Etheridge smiled again.

"And," continued his wife, "while she stood at my knee, Gertrude glided to her side, and stole her arm round her sister's waist. The little five year old caught each sound and echoed it." 'May I soon go to school, mamma?' asked Bertha, 'and I, too?' chimed in Gertrude; and while we were discussing the 'wherefores and why nots' of the matter, up to the closed venetian door, steals my baby boy, escaped from the nursery, with 'mamma, if you'll let me in, I'll give you a very sweet kiss!'"

"Did you open the door?" asked Mr. Etheridge.

"I ran to the door," continued Mary, "I opened

it, I stooped, and with his dear soft, young arms around my neck, I received the promised embrace. What a treasure he is, my dear, so sweet, so noble, so bright and beautiful, my lovely boy!"

" *Your* boy, indeed!" said Mr. Etheridge, rising suddenly on his elbow, and looking full in the face of his wife, "your boy, indeed! did you not sell to me all your right and interest in that child, before his birth, with the express understanding that you should never again suffer the pains, and indure the trials of that interesting period?"

"Oh, my darling!" said Mary, while a crimson blush dyed her countenance; "surely I never made you such a promise."

"It is true, it is true!" said her husband, looking mischievously in her eyes; "it seems to me your memory is entirely too convenient."

Sitting down by the side of his wife, he took her white hands in his, the hands he had so lovingly and proudly jewel-decked, and pressing them in his own, and contrasting them with his so bronzed by the sun, he said, while a father's pride and glory shone full in his face:

"Yes, my wife, thank God, our children give great promise, every one of them. Upon you falls the principal charge of their education, and it is not necessary for me to say, how fully, how entirely I trust in you to make them excellent men and women, should God spare us all, and how confident I am of your success.

"It is my greatest desire, next to seeing them Christians, that they shall be thoroughly and elegantly educated, and as I have ample means at my disposal, for which I humbly and gratefully thank God, I shall spare no effort, no expense, no. perseverance to accomplish that object. I dined to-day with Mr. and Mrs. Lincoln, and we had a long conversation on the subject. Mrs. Lincoln talked much of all the children, and I scarcely know which one she likes best."

"Mother is very much attached to them all," said Mary, "and they love her devotedly."

Mary sank into a reverie, Mr. Etheridge still at her feet.

Her thoughts were fixed on Gertrude and Mrs. Day, who were preparing to go to Europe with their father and husband. Mary almost envied them, for her desire to see the works of art and of nature, of which she had so often read, was intense.

At present she, too, "nursed the mighty project," but did not see much hope of its fulfillment.

Mr. Etheridge again took his wife's hand caressingly in his, and soon touching the plain gold ring of the fourth finger, he said:

"What ring is *this* ?"

"The ring which has never left my finger since the memorable evening on which you placed it there, with these words : 'With this ring, I thee,' etc., and when you promised to 'love and cherish me.'" said she, stooping over, and imprinting a kiss on his brow, "and I promised to ' obey,' which promise I have faithfully kept and performed ever since that time."

"You have, indeed! have you?" laughed Mr. Ethe-

20

ridge, jumping to his feet, "tell me *when* you have obeyed, and where."

"One would judge from your tone," playfully pouted Mary, "that I never had obeyed you in all my life, and I am sure I never disobeyed, did I? To tell you the truth," said she, speaking seriously, "and I have often dwelt upon it, I do not believe, my love, that you ever gave me an order; our days have flowed on together so harmoniously, blended as it were in one, all our thoughts and wishes coincided so entirely; in truth it is remarkable, is it not my husband?"

Mr. Etheridge stooped to the low chair in which his wife sat, and drew her up tenderly, and out through the open door, into the porch, flooded by moonlight, and under the sweet-scented vine blossoms, he folded her to his bosom, and he told her how more than position, than wealth, than health, than life itself, she was to him. And as the tender eloquent words of her husband fell like richest melody on her heart, calling up the happy blush to her cheek, she looked back, back, to far-off years, she saw her dead mother in that well-remembered chamber; her other mother, the alienation of her beloved father, her youthful trials and sorrows, the griefs, the withered hopes of later years, she looked off into the moonlight, and far up into the sky, and her heart sang its anthem of praise and thanksgiving to God for all His mercies, for His wonderful goodness to her and hers, for her noble father's returned love, for her mother's affection, her husband's tenderness, her children's devotion, and the esteem of true friends. And as she gazed into heaven, heaven filled her soul, her being.

And he who stood beside her, and looked into her mild beaming eyes, he, too, sang to great Heaven his silent song of gratitude and of glory.

And the moon shone down upon that true-hearted man, and his true-hearted wife, and the overshadowing vine leaves danced in the soft summer-evening air.